THE FLETCHER

Clan Ross of the Hebrides

Copyright © 2023 by Hildie McQueen
Print Edition

All rights reserved. No part of this book may be reproduced in any form or by any electronic or mechanical means—except in the case of brief quotations embodied in critical articles or reviews—without written permission.

The characters and events portrayed in this book are fictitious. Any similarity to real persons, living or dead, is purely coincidental and not intended by the author.

ISBN: 978-1-960608-00-0

Also By Hildie McQueen

Clan Ross of the Hebrides
The Lion: Darach
The Beast: Duncan
The Eagle: Stuart
The Fox: Caelan
The Stag: Artair
The Wildcat: Gideon
The Hunter: Ella's Story (Novella)
The Fletcher: Padriag
The Duke: Clan Ross Prequel

Clan Ross Series
A Heartless Laird
A Hardened Warrior
A Hellish Highlander
A Flawed Scotsman
A Fearless Rebel
A Fierce Archer

Guards of the Hebrides
Erik
Torac
Struan

Moriag Series
Beauty and the Highlander
The Lass and the Laird
Lady and the Scot
The Laird's Daughter

Clan Ross of the Hebrides

This fictional story takes place at the beginning of the 17th century in the Scottish Hebrides, isles off the Isle of Skye's western coasts.

In the 1500s, lordship over the Hebrides collapsed and the power was given to clan chiefs: The MacNeil, in Barra; The Macdonald (Clanranald), in South Uist; The Uisdein, in North Uist; The MacLeod, the isles of Harris and Lewis.

For this series, I have moved the clans around a bit to help the story work better. The clans' locations in my books are as follows. The MacNeil will remain in Barra. The Macdonald (Clanranald) is moved to North Uist. The Uisdein resides in Benbecula. The MacLeod remains in the isles of Harris and Lewis. My fictional clan, Clan Ross, will laird over South Uist.

CHAPTER ONE

1603, North Uist, Isle of the Hebrides

THE WILD WIND whipped around so hard, Padraig Macdonald wondered if it would sweep him from his steed. Like some sort of warning, the weather was not cooperating as he and his men galloped over the uneven terrain of North Uist, away from his clan's lands to MacLeod territory.

Although not exactly riding off to battle, he and the warriors were extra vigilant. Just a few days earlier, there had been a clash between MacLeod and the Macdonald clansmen over land both laid claim to.

In truth, there were many places the border was uneven, and it was hard to distinguish which clan the land belonged to. Over the years, the lairds had been lenient in regard to it. However, as of late, the MacLeod clan had become proprietary about ownership of the areas near the border between their lands.

As a result of the last clash, there had been one death—a Macdonald—and plenty of injuries on both sides.

Evander, Padraig's older brother and the clan's laird, immediately dispatched him and his men to patrol the area to ensure their people's safety.

As they rounded the loch's edge, Padraig became painfully aware of the lack of any tall vegetation. There were no trees behind which they could seek shelter or hide if the need arose. There were only a collection of hills in the distance. It was only there, at the base of the hills, that he and his men could be concealed from anyone coming from MacLeod lands.

It was late summer and already the weather had begun to cool. Perhaps a pair of hours of daylight remained and Padraig—preferring to avoid sleeping out in the elements—decided he and his men should return to the Macdonald keep before nightfall. With his gaze on the surroundings, he urged his mount to the safety of the foothills.

Padraig lifted his arm and immediately the men quieted. "We are on MacLeod lands, so I will remind ye: Do not make a move first. Keep yer weapons shielded. Draw yer sword only if there is no doubt it is required."

After another hour, as Padraig was about to give the order to return, when a group of warriors appeared in the distance. The riders came from the direction of the shoreline.

"Remain here," Padraig stated to his men. "Except you two." He motioned for two warriors to move forward and flank him on both sides.

The riders who approached were undoubtedly MacLeods, their wary gazes moving from Padraig to the men behind him. "We head to see the Macdonald. Our laird, the MacLeod, wishes to meet with yers immediately," a bearded thick-necked man stated. "He invites him to come to Harris."

"No need to travel further. I will give him the message," Padraig replied keeping his gaze flat. I am his brother, Padraig Macdonald. What assurance do we have of safe passage?"

The MacLeod warriors exchanged a look. "He will be safe. My laird gives his word."

"My brother will send a messenger with his decision."

LAIRD EVANDER MACDONALD sat back in thought after Padraig relayed the message from the men they'd run into. After their father lost his battle to a prolonged illness, Evander had taken his place. He'd only been laird for a short time and was still becoming accustomed to the myriad of responsibilities.

"The MacLeod lives on the Isle of Harris. He expects me to travel there," Evander said, seeming to be thinking out loud.

Padraig spoke up, "It would be dangerous, especially if he is planning some sort of attack."

"That is a possibility," his brother replied with a huff. "I will consider it for a few days before deciding what to do."

"What of the border lands?" Rauri Macdonald, their cousin, asked. "Our people are not safe."

That the MacLeod claimed the northern portion of North Uist as MacLeod territory had been a thorn in their father's side for years and now it was Evander's problem to deal with.

The MacLeod refused to give the land up. In his defense, the people who lived there were MacLeods. Unfortunately, they were also very proprietary and often fought with anyone who dared to cross what they considered to be the border.

"Talks of a truce have always been fruitless," Padraig stated. "Father spoke to the Macleod several times and here we are, back to them attacking people."

The sound of voices in the great room signaled it was time for last meal.

Evander stood and stretched. "Did his men return to Harris?"

"Nay,"—Padraig shook his head—"they stated they would not leave and will await yer reply at the shoreline."

"I will dispatch a messenger letting him know when we will travel there. I will ask that in response, he order his men to keep our people safe near the borderlands. We will see what the MacLeod's reply is."

They did not have a high board at the Macdonald keep. The late laird had been unable to stand easily and therefore sat at a lower table and Evander kept the custom. Instead of a high board, the family's table was at the front of the room. Four long tables in straight lines were placed lengthwise so that whenever the laird wished to address the room, those in attendance could turn their head and see him.

Padraig held out a chair for his mother, Lady Aileen Macdonald, who kissed his cheek before sitting. He then lowered into a chair so that his mother was on his right and Evander on his left. To Evander's left was his wife, Ella Ross Macdonald.

Although Rauri was family and had every right to join them at the head table, the warrior preferred to sit with the guards. Unless there was an important visitor, then he would sit at the family table.

As the meal progressed, his mother touched Padraig's arm. "Have ye considered who to marry? Laird MacAulay and his family are to visit in the next sennight. He has two daughters of marriageable age, ye know?"

"I have not given marriage any thought. There is no need for me to marry. Evander has given ye two grandchildren already."

His mother gave Padraig a pointed look. "Ye will marry, I will ensure it. Marriage will settle ye and stop all the running about with a different woman every night."

Pressing his lips to keep from laughing, he gave his mother a pointed look. "I have ceased to *run about* for a while now. Have ye not noticed? I have settled on my own."

His mother's eyes narrowed. "The maid, Penny, told the cook that ye and she… Well, ye know."

Why did women talk so much? Padraig shrugged. "I am not a priest. A man has desires."

"Keep yer desires away from the servants. We cannot have a chambermaid mooning over ye when the laird's daughters arrive."

He lowered his voice and spoke into his mother's ear. "She came to my bedchamber and climbed into my bed. It is them ye should chastise."

"Bah!" his mother replied. "Stole yer virtue did she?"

Padraig let out a long sigh and turned to Evander. "Distract Mother."

His brother shook his head. By the smirk on his face, he'd overheard the conversation. "Ye got yerself into this. When I was unmarried, I stayed away from the household maids when seeking bedsport."

"Distract her from wishing to marry me off. I do not wish to be tied down anytime soon." Padraig slid a look around the room. There were plenty of single, attractive women in the clan and if he married, he would like to marry someone who was already a member of their clan. He had absolutely no desire to bring someone into the fold who would be pining for her home and family constantly.

"What if ye have to marry a MacLeod?" Evander studied his face. "It could be the perfect way to instill a permanent truce."

The blood in his veins turned to ice. "A... MacLeod?" His eyes rounded and his ability to speak left him. To marry anyone related to that man was a fate worse than death.

Padriag gave Evander a narrowed look. "Why of course, dear brother. There is nothing I wish for more than marrying a woman who could possibly kill me in my sleep."

Evander lifted a brow. "I doubt it will not come to that. However, we do have to consider all options to ensure peace."

The food on his plate lost its appeal. So instead, he lifted the cup of ale and drained it. Once again he studied the people in the room. Everyone was familiar. There were the clansmen who'd come to speak to the laird about issues with land or with other clans, their guards, and some who'd come to ask for asylum and were now housed there. He wondered how a newcomer would see his clan.

When the meal ended, he caught up to Ella who walked out of the great room. The woman was a perfect fit for his brother. Independent and opinionated, she stood up to his temperamental brother and was the only one who could calm him whenever his famous tempter erupted.

"How fare ye Padraig?" Ella asked looking to him. "It seems yer mother is intent on getting ye married off." Her statement made it obvious that Evander had told her what they'd spoken about. "I remember Mother doing the same with my brothers. They were always annoyed about it."

"It is not that I do not wish to marry. I do not understand why suddenly it is so important to her."

Ella shrugged. "Must be that she wishes to see ye settled." Her eyes danced playfully as she slid a look to the servants cleaning up the great room.

Letting out a breath, Padraig took her elbow. "May I ask ye a question?"

"Of course." Ella allowed him to lead her out to the courtyard.

"I know ye visited the keep many times while growing up. Once ye came to live here, how did ye feel about the keep and the people?"

The lovely woman scanned the surroundings as if seeing them for the first time. "As I came here often, I suppose there was little that surprised me. However, I must admit to always finding the keep so very beautiful. It is like none other."

Ella's lips curved into a soft smile. "I find it beautiful, surprising, and inviting. I would say anyone seeing it for the first time would think that. However, upon seeing the surrounding wall with guards atop and sentries at the gates, those considering any kind of ill would think twice before advancing."

Indeed, the home had been built away from the village, but still accessible by wagon or on foot. The structure was made of white stones, giving the keep a dramatic appearance as it stood out from the surrounding landscape.

His ancestors had it built, so Padraig had grown up there his entire life. Therefore, it could be said that he found other keeps with their dull gray walls to be austere and uninviting, while his home was bright. No expense had been spared for the furnishings but like the outside, his family had always leaned toward lighter woods and colors.

"And the people?" Padraig inquired. "Do ye think a newcomer, from another clan, would be welcome?"

"It depends," Ella said giving him a curious look. "Much like any clan, people here are wary of newcomers. Why do ye ask?"

He shrugged. "Considering how things would be if it happens that I am forced to marry a MacLeod."

"A MacLeod?" Her eyes rounded. "I surely hope not. I can speak to Evander if ye wish?"

Padraig tracked a flock of gulls that flew toward the seashore. "It is not necessary. I do not think it will come to that."

Needing to distract himself, he went to the archer's quarters. Several men sat about making arrows. One motioned to an empty stool. "The best fletcher of all graces us with his presence."

"Ye are thankful that I do when ye reach in yer quiver for one I made," Padraig said as he lowered to the stool and began working. The making of arrows required attention and patience. It was the perfect way to relax while doing something useful. It was arrows that fed families and defended against enemies.

CHAPTER TWO

THE SLAP CAUSED Freya MacLeod to stumble sideways and her hands automatically went up to protect herself from another strike.

"Get yerself out of here. I tire of yer impertinence," her stepmother hissed. "It is ruined because of ye."

Freya straightened, lifted her chin, and glared at Orla MacLeod, the miserable woman whom her father had deemed a suitable wife after her mother's death. "I have never been taught how to stain fabric. Ye should not have asked me to do it."

"Leave!" This time Orla didn't bother keeping her voice low. "Get out of my sight ye stupid, stupid lass."

Knowing it would anger the woman further, Freya shrugged and took her time walking out of the room. It was exhausting having to put up with the woman's constant demeaning treatment and no one to stand up for her. As of late, the only one Freya could count on was herself.

Her father's head lifted when she walked into his study. Surrounded by parchments, maps, and the ever-present decanter of whisky, he was in his element.

"What is it this time Freya?" There was no warmth in his voice, more of a bored tone.

"She struck me." Freya met his gaze. "Next time I will hit

her back."

Her father let out a sigh. "Ye will do no such thing. She is yer mother—"

"She is *not* my mother."

Her father's gaze went to her face probably noting the red mark from the slap. He sounded tired. "Avoid her Freya. I will not be bothered with these hysterics. Keep away from her and try not to be troubling."

Freya walked closer to the table he sat at. Peering down at the maps she noticed that he'd scribbled notes along a thick line that had been drawn. Macdonald was written several times.

"Are we battling with them again?"

The last time there had been a battle between the Macdonalds and the MacLeods, it had been horrible. Neither side had gained anything, and both had lost plenty of men.

She continued, "I thought that when they allied with the MacLeods of Lewis, we too became allies."

Her father met her gaze. "Freya, I will not discuss clan matters with a lass. Go and find something to do." He waved his hand dismissively.

"I will go for a walk," she informed him knowing his attention was back to his maps and such.

As of late, her life had become frustrating. The only thing that kept her sane was her plan to leave. She walked out of her father's study, grabbed a cloak from a hook near the side door, and hurried outside, then headed to Coombe, the local village.

Her destination took her down a path alongside the keep, then a short distance through the woods. It was late afternoon and the fresh air of the surroundings helped to clear her mind.

Upon arriving at the nearby village, only a few shops remained open. Freya hurried into one before anyone caught sight of her. It would not do to be reported back to her family. Mostly she feared being found missing and earn the ire of the wretched Orla.

Then again her stepmother would mostly likely think she was in her bedchamber and no one else should seek her out for the rest of the day.

"Ah, there ye are lass." Eva, the shopkeeper, smiled showing her missing front teeth. The older woman gave her a pat on her shoulder. "Ye are such a bright young thing."

At the touch and words of encouragement, Freya sighed. It was sad that someone like Eva was one of the few to show her kindness.

"I have some coin for ye. The bundles of herbs ye make, for stomach ailments, have sold out. Ye should bring more."

Freya accepted the coins and then paid the woman her portion. "Thank ye. I will do that." She shoved the coins into a pocket hidden in the folds of her skirt. "Is there anything else I should bring?"

The woman motioned to a crudely made wooden cross on a stand that Freya had made to hang leather necklaces from. "There are only three left."

"I doubt many more will sell. There are only so many people in the village. Everyone must have one by now." Freya lifted the three necklaces she'd taken painstaking time to make. The leather had been cut into fine strips, then she'd braided them. "I will make a few more."

"What will ye do with yer coin?" Eva asked. "Ye never buy anything for yerself. Yer clothes are yer stepsister's discarded ones."

Freya laughed. "My attire is not important to me. I did get a new pair of frocks recently. And new shoes. I suspect my stepmother was forced to do it because we are to have guests."

"Are they to marry ye off then?"

The question struck her silent. It made sense, as they'd never taken any kind of interest in her clothes or shoes before. This time, however, Orla had been insistent that she have the articles made.

She shrugged. "I doubt it. I will return in three days," Freya told Eva as she walked out of the shop, hurried around to the back, and dashed through the trees back to the keep.

UNLIKE THE MACLEODS of Lewis, her father's lands were much smaller and less impressive. The keep was a good size, but from what she'd learned, it was modest when compared to most.

Her uncle, the laird of the MacLeods of Lewis, was powerful and had a large army of men. Because of it, her father often overstepped and fought against clans much larger than theirs. He counted on the fact his brother would step in and protect him.

In Freya's opinion, it was not very valiant or impressive. She hated war and detested strife between her family and other people. It was the clan's people who suffered when battles happened. For the most part, her own family was not affected.

Arriving at the keep, she hurried through the gates and went to the side door that led into the kitchens. The aroma drew her into the small space, and Freya went to one of the bubbling pots and peered into it.

"Goat stew," Annis, the cook said behind her. "Would ye like some?"

"Yes, thank ye," Freya replied with a bright smile. "I have something for ye. I went to see Eva. Every bundle we made sold." Freya took two coins and gave them to the woman whose eyes widened in delight. "Ye do not have to give me coin Miss Freya. I will help ye make more bundles free of charge."

"Ye are the only one who cares about me in this household. Besides, I know how much ye need it."

The woman's face fell. "If only yer mother were still here. She would be so proud of ye." Her eyes went to the doorway. "If only."

"We cannot do anything about it," Freya said sitting down, her mouth watering in anticipation.

While she ate, she told Annis about the new clothes. "Why do ye think she had new clothes made for me?"

Annis shook her head. "Let us hope that if it is because ye are to be married off, that it be to a good man who will treat ye fairly."

"If it is a good man who's coming here, she will be shoving Iona forward, not me. I do not have a good feeling about this."

"Let us pray this is all for good," Annis said, not sounding at all convincing.

"It matters not," Freya replied. "I have a plan."

"Lass. Do not do anything rash."

UNLIKE THE REST of the family, who slept on the second floor, Freya's bedchamber was on the first floor, down the hall from the kitchen. It was small and simply furnished, but she adored it. A window opened to a view of the loch and brought fresh air into the space. She had a bed that was comfortable and a dressing table and mirror that had been her mother's. Along the wall she had a washstand with a pitcher and bowl that had also belonged to her mother.

The room was fragrant as she kept baskets filled with herbs that she'd cut when taking walks in the forest and cuttings from the garden she'd planted just outside her window.

Baskets and wrapped bundles of herbs were neatly stacked along the opposite wall of her bed. On the floor was a thick woven blanket that she'd folded in half to provide comfort when she sat and worked on her herb bundles and sachets. Her mother had left pages of notes for healing herbs that she'd found one day when going through items in a closet.

In her bedchamber, Freya felt her mother's presence. Every item that she'd touched, every item that she used, were treasures that she clung to.

Upon marrying her father, Orla had removed most of his late wife's belongings from sight. Freya had taken as many as she could and kept them in her room. A tapestry embroidered by her mother hung over her headboard. Small trinkets lay on a side table. Her mother's favorite shawl was neatly folded over the back of a chair.

After securing the door to ensure no one entered, Freya kneeled and pulled a rug over to the side in order to reveal a loose floorboard. Lifting the short plank, Freya took out a small wooden box that had been a gift from her parents. Digging in her pocket, she grasped the coins left after paying Eva and sharing with Annis.

Tink. Tink. The coins fell atop the others in the box. There was more than enough for her to start anew.

She studied the contents. The box was filled to the rim with coins. In the small opening, along with the box, there was a small leather drawstring purse that also held coins. It was small and had filled up quickly, so she'd added the box. Years of savings meant she'd reached her goal to fill the box. Only a few more coins would fit before spilling over.

Freya's lips curved at her accomplishment. That she'd managed to acquire such an impressive amount on her own made her proud. Her mother would be astonished at her ingenuity.

After carefully placing the box back next to the pouch and replacing the plank and the rug, she stretched out on her stomach atop her bed. She began making a mental list of what to take when leaving and going far away.

In preparation for when the right time presented itself, there was already a satchel with some necessary items in it.

Since the satchel had been on the floor next to the dressing table for so long no one was curious about it. If anyone peeked inside, they'd see things that would not pique their interest. In it she'd placed a few small things that had belonged to her mother. A handkerchief, a scarf, a comb, and a pendant. They were all bundled together, wrapped in a scrap of linen. A neatly folded chemise, a pair of stockings, and a frock were also packed inside.

There was still enough room left for another dress and any belongings she couldn't bear to leave behind.

Her gaze slid to the new clothes that hung from wooden pegs. Both dresses were the same simple style, with square bodices and long flowing skirts. One was a pale grey and the other a deep brown.

Turning her mind to what had occurred earlier, she sighed. In truth she did wish to learn to die fabric. Unaware of the need to constantly stir the fabric in the large tub with the wooden paddle, all she'd done was push it into the water. It had turned out splotched with varying shades of hue. Though if one were to ask her—it looked rather interesting.

Iona, Orla's daughter, had been in tears as the fabric was meant to be for her new dress, so she had run off to complain to her mother.

Freya rolled her eyes. It wasn't as if Iona did not have something to wear already. It seemed every time the wind blew Iona would get a new frock.

Her mind returned to the subject at hand when the perfect time would be to escape and get away from there. No matter what Annis said, she had no doubt that the only reason she'd be married off was to get her out of the way. It would not be a profitable match or anything to do with gain for the family. It was also possible that it was a way for her stepmother to get rid of her.

Waiting until well after last meal ended, Freya left her bedchamber and went in search of her father. To her annoyance, he sat in the parlor with his wife and Iona.

Orla glared at her obviously irritated at her presence.

"Ye were not at last meal," her father stated.

Since it was not a question Freya refrained from replying. Instead she remained standing. "Is someone expected to visit soon?"

"Aye," her father started, but was interrupted by his wife.

"Never ye mind." Orla slid a look to Iona. "It has nothing

to do with ye."

Her father shrugged. "It is not a secret dear. The Macdonald and his brother should arrive in the next day or two. I trust ye will make yerself presentable." His gaze scanned over her and by his contrite expression, found her lacking.

"I had new dresses made for both of them," Orla said, in an overly sweet tone. "If she dresses as she does, it is her choice."

Orla slid another look to Iona, then to Freya. "I will not be embarrassed by ye as I am considering a possible match for yer sister."

"Of course she will dress presentably, won't ye Freya?" her father asked.

"Aye," Freya replied and sat in a chair.

Iona's face went from sour at Freya's decision to remain in the room to a wide smile. "Am I to be matched to Padraig Macdonald?"

It was well established that Laird Evander's brother, Padraig, was very handsome. Although Freya had only caught sight of him once at the games, she'd never forgotten his face. Despite knowing she'd never be matched with someone like him, it still angered her that Iona would be considered for such a man.

Just to annoy her stepmother, she gave her father a pointed look. "I am eldest and therefore should be matched first. Mother would be displeased."

At the mention of her mother, the laird looked to his wife. "Of-of course. It is just that they asked for Iona, specifically."

She'd learned to recognize her father's expressions when he lied. And he'd just lied, but Freya let it pass.

The temporary look of astonishment in her stepmother's

face was enough of a reward for her. "I suppose if that is what truly happened, then I cannot object. I do look forward to meeting the Macdonalds."

"I do not see what ye could possibly say to them. Ye have nothing of interest in yer life," Iona snapped. "Ye should stay away from them." She had the nerve to cross her arms and pout.

"Do ye see?" Orla said. "Freya relishes causing distress, ruining a perfectly relaxing evening."

Although Freya managed a bored expression before getting up and turning away to leave, the statement stung. That they never included her hurt deeply. What made it worse was that her father didn't seem to notice—or care.

THE NEXT MORNING'S cool breeze woke Freya, and she dressed in an old frock, stockings, and worn shoes. Then she plopped down on the floor and finished putting her bundles together to take to the village.

She'd decided to slip away to the village that day. It would be a perfect time. With the visitors coming, her father would not miss her. Besides, the sooner she could collect more money, the sooner she could plan her escape.

The sounds of servant's voices outside made her stand and look out the window.

"What happens?" she asked a chambermaid, who carried a basket of linens from the clotheslines.

"The visitors arrive." Her playful gaze met Freya's. "Yer family is not awake yet."

It was late morning, which meant her father and mother had stayed up late drinking, as per usual.

"Perfect," Freya replied smiling back. She hurriedly threw the herb bundles and sachets in a basket and went to greet the visitors.

THE MACDONALD WAS escorted by ten men. Freya motioned for the guards to open the gates and walked out.

After an exaggerated curtsy, she looked up at the two men who rode in front. She knew who the Macdonald was as she'd seen him before. And if she hadn't known him, it was obvious by the fact he wore a traditional plaid that was pinned in place with the clan crest. He was ruggedly handsome—one could almost say intimidating—except for the fact her father was one of the most unapproachable men on the isles, so she found it hard to be affected.

"Welcome Laird," Freya called out. "I trust yer travels were unremarkable."

"They were," the laird replied.

The man on the laird's right looked down from his steed. Her gaze lifted to his and her breath caught.

The Macdonald was ruggedly handsome, but this man was absolutely breathtaking. With bright blue eyes and dark brown hair that fell in waves to his shoulders, he was astonishingly attractive. He had to be Padraig Macdonald.

"Who are ye lass?"

"I am Freya Macdonald." She looked over her shoulder to note her father hurrying out to stand just outside the doorway. "Ah, there is my Da now."

With a chuckle, she stood aside as they rode past blocking her from view and she quickly walked down the well-worn path. No doubt her father had not noticed her, probably too busy wondering why they'd arrived so early. Then he'd figure out it wasn't early and pretend to have been occupied and not sleeping.

There was a curious sound from behind. Freya slowed and looked over her shoulder, almost screaming at seeing a man so close behind her.

It took a few seconds to realize it was Padraig.

"What is it?" she snapped, annoyed that he'd followed. The more distance she placed between them the better. It was easy to be bitter at Iona getting to marry such a handsome man, while she'd probably be given away to an old ugly one.

"Where are ye headed?" His brilliant gaze met hers, sending shivers of awareness down her spine.

"To the village," Freya replied hiking her chin. "To take these to the herb shop."

He peered at the pitiful items in her basket. "What are they?"

"Ye really should return to the keep. My father is rather eager to introduce ye to my sister, Iona."

"What are they?" he repeated, seeming not to hear what she'd just said.

"Herb bundles, they are to be boiled and the brew will alleviate an upset stomach. The satchels can be boiled for settling nerves or sniffed for the same reason." She held one out to him. "Here. Ye may need this for when ye meet Iona."

He took the satchel and gave her a puzzled look. "Why are ye selling herbs? Are ye not the MacLeod's youngest daughter?"

"I am the eldest and I do it to earn coin. I really must go." She swung around and hurried away listening intently in case he followed.

Freya wasn't sure if she wished he would or wished he would not to the keep.

CHAPTER THREE

Pulling his stead behind, Padraig made his way back through the gates and into the courtyard. The large area was well kept, but he did not release his horse to the lads who hurried to fetch him. One of them gave him a startled look when he held on to the reins.

"Ensure he is kept in the corral for now. Ye may give him water and oats. I will be there shortly to remove his saddle and brush him down."

"We can do that sir," one of the lads exclaimed. Seeming rather small to be a stable worker, Padraig wondered if he could handle his war horse. "There is no need. He is temperamental and I do not wish him to cause injury."

Once the lads left with the horse, he turned his attention to the group gathered in front of the arched doorway.

The MacLeod was older than he remembered, next to him was a woman who Padraig assumed was his wife. Beside her was a young woman who looked very different from Freya. This daughter was blonde with sharp angular features. Her lips were pressed together, her pointed gaze looking him over from head to toe as if assessing his value.

When he approached, she hitched her pointy chin and gave him a wide smile. Padraig pretended not to notice.

"Where did ye go?" Laird MacLeod asked when they were

introduced.

"I had to ensure my horse did not have a stone lodged. He walked a bit awkwardly. It could be the ride on the birlinn on the way here that had him a bit unbalanced."

Evander slid a look to him but didn't say anything. Padraig wasn't sure why he didn't state he had met Freya. It was probable her father would not be keen on the idea of her going to the village alone.

"Please, come in. Ye are welcome." The laird motioned to a wide doorway. They walked into the great room where servants scurried about preparing a table for them.

"I apologize for our lack of preparation," Lady MacLeod said, her gaze snapping toward the servants. "Every one of them will be admonished. They were ordered to have everything ready, but ye see…" She trailed off motioning to the room.

First, they would eat and drink, speak of nonconsequential things, and then linger even longer while the laird gave them a tour of the land and stables. Finally, they would speak about the purpose of the visit. It was the way things were done and as much as both he and Evander did not wish to remain for more than a day, they would have to.

It was interesting that throughout the meal, neither the laird nor his wife seemed to notice the eldest daughter was missing. On the contrary, it was as if all was normal.

Lady MacLeod doted on her daughter, Iona, pointing out every quality the lass possessed. Obviously the woman did her best to present the lass as a valuable asset. Whether the MacLeod considered a connection between them to be fortuitous was not as obvious.

Finally, the laird invited Evander to go outside. Padraig stood as well, but Lady MacLeod stopped him with a hand on his arm. "Would ye mind terribly going with Iona to the garden? She wishes to cut flowers to decorate the tables for last meal. I cannot accompany her as ye may expect, I must ensure all is well in the kitchens."

Padraig pressed his back teeth together. "I am not sure it is a good idea for such a lovely lass to be seen alone with a man."

"Ye, girl. Come here." The woman motioned to a startled servant girl who'd been sweeping the soot from the fireplace. "Walk with them. Keep yer distance."

The girl bobbed and looked to him and Iona with expectation.

Iona turned on her heel. "My personal maid is unwell," she said walking to the front door. Padraig and the young servant hurried to catch up.

"I do not care for much sun on my face. Ye do not know my stepsister, but she has a horrible, freckled face from it…"

As the woman kept talking, Padraig remained silent. Not only because she barely took a breath between sentences, but also because it gave him time to study the area and note places where it would be easy to escape if the need arose.

"Where is this sister of yers?" he asked nonchalantly.

The servant's eyes rounded, and Padraig realized the lass knew where Freya had gone.

Iona waved a hand dismissively. "I do not know. Father told her she had to be present today. Obviously she did not obey. She even got a new dress."

The servant girl rolled her eyes and turned to look away in the direction Freya had gone.

When a long time passed and Iona had not picked one flower, Padraig was ready to yank some from the ground. She'd not stopped talking the entire time. Currently she told him about meeting a famous traveling bard who'd composed a song upon meeting her.

"His voice was like nothing I've ever heard," she continue. "I only wish I would have committed the song to memory. Though I do think someone may have written it down."

"Ye have not picked any flowers," Padraig stated. "Ye did not bring a basket."

Iona turned to the servant girl. "Pick some flowers."

The servant frowned, looked around, and began pinching blooms. Padraig almost laughed when he saw she was picking weeds while trying to listen to what was said between him and Iona.

Iona paused midsentence as the laird came into view, walking from the stables. Padraig jumped at the chance to leave. "I must see about my steed. I will leave ye to it." He walked away before the woman could stop him.

"I WILL CUT my own throat if ye even suggest that I marry her," Padraig hissed a few moments later when he and Evander had excused themselves to speak to their men. They crossed the courtyard to where their ten guards stood about watching the MacLeod warriors practice.

It was obvious the display was set up on purpose to either impress or intimidate. By the Macdonald men's bored expressions, neither occurred.

"Rauri," Evander said motioning their cousin over. "How are things?"

The wide-shouldered male shrugged. "Seems they are too busy trying to impress with swordplay to be bothered with us. The gates are kept open for villagers. The men who are patrolling are keeping an eye, but for the most part seem unconcerned.

"I will ride out to the bìrlinns to ensure all is well there," Padraig stated, anxious to be away from any opportunity Iona would take to seek him out.

Upon fetching his still saddled horse, he and another warrior rode out through the gates. His brother did not feel there was a need to inform the MacLeod of their decision to check on the warriors. After all, it was his right to ensure the safety of the men.

Padraig kept his mount from going too fast, as he was unfamiliar with the rocky expanse of the isle. Unlike near his home on North Uist, the land here had plenty of sharp-edged craggy hills that required care, so the horse's hooves didn't get caught.

They found both bìrlinns still tethered and the half dozen guards sitting around a bonfire roasting meat and laughing about something someone said.

The men waved to Padraig and his companion cheerfully.

Upon nearing, Padraig realized why the men were in such good spirits. A short distance away, a group of curious women had gathered. Some washed clothes, others gave up pretending to be there for a reason and just stood near a cusp of trees looking over.

"Do not let yer guard down when ye lower ye breeches," Padraig said looking toward where the women.

After a while, Padraig rode back to the MacLeod keep. He

considered that perhaps the eldest sister, Freya, would attend last meal. That the MacLeod cared little for his daughter was surprising, as she was a true MacLeod, unlike Iona.

It was also obvious that with regard to the daughters, his wife controlled which one was presented to visitors.

Upon arriving at the keep, he unsaddled and brushed his horse before guiding it to a stall in the stables. From the corner of his eye, he caught sight of Freya. She slipped into the courtyard through a gate in the far corner, partially hidden by a cart and sacks of grain.

Once past the stables, she walked nonchalantly toward the house.

Padraig hurried to catch up with her. "I trust yer business went well."

When she smiled up at him, something in his stomach tumbled. She had the most beautiful brown eyes, with golden specks, framed by thick lashes. In the center of her chin, a slight indentation invited one to press a kiss there.

There was a smudge of mud on the left side of her face that made her even more adorable. "It went well, thank ye for asking. If ye would excuse me, I must hurry inside." She motioned to a doorway just ahead. "The kitchen entrance."

"Will ye be at last meal?" Padraig hoped her reply would be yes.

She sighed. "I do not have a choice, so aye."

"Ye seem to keep separate from yer family. Why?" He found that he did not wish her to go away but to continue speaking to him.

Her brows knitted together as she studied him. "Come." Side-by-side, they made their way around the side of the house to a small garden.

"This is my private garden where I plant my herbs," Freya explained. "Mint, lavender, rosemary, chamomile…" Her words trailed off. "I am not sure why I'm telling ye this. Ye probably have little interest."

Padraig looked around the tidy garden. "I am impressed by yer work and find ye a refreshing change from most lasses I've met."

"I do this because keeping to myself is preferable to being…" She stopped talking. "Father is content to be in the company of Orla and Iona, I am happy for him."

She'd not answered the question. Not directly. However, Padraig got the idea she'd accepted her place and was not unhappy. There was a peaceful air about her that set him at ease.

"Has Orla tried to match ye up with Iona yet?"

"I am not here to be matched," Padraig replied, a bit more curtly than he meant to. "My brother and I came to speak to yer father about the border between our lands on North Uist."

Freya studied him for a long moment. "I hope the issue gets resolved; I am sure father will be cooperative. He has become more agreeable as of late."

She lowered to a bench and looked across the short grassy area to the loch. When he lowered to sit next to her, she slid a look to him but did not speak. For a few moments they sat in amicable silence.

He tried but could not recall ever sitting with a woman like this. Relaxed, no other plan than to take in the view before them. With Freya it was as if they'd known each other and were comfortable without having to fill the quiet spaces with words.

Admittedly, at the same time, he was wildly attracted to her. He wanted to know more about the woman. Strange that he put getting to know someone over seduction, but he decided there was always a first time for everything.

There was something very different about the lass.

"My mother loved to sit and look at the loch. We would often sit together in silence, just like now."

"What happened to her?" Padraig studied Freya's profile noting she didn't seem to be bothered by the question.

Her lips curved. "She fell asleep one night and did not wake. Father's distraught calls awakened the entire household. I rushed to their bedchamber as the healer was called." She hesitated to take in a deep breath. "There was nothing to be done."

"Last meal will be served shortly. I must change or face the wrath of Orla," Freya said looking down at her faded clothes. "I will see ye then." With that she stood and briskly walked back the way they'd come.

Padraig remained just a bit longer. The lass was like no one he'd known before. Spoke about matters that would bring most women to tears with the clarity of acceptance that surprised him.

He liked her.

Last meal was sure to be an ordeal. He planned to sit with Rauri and the other guards in an effort to stay as far away from Iona as possible.

When he entered the great room, Evander stood by the fireplace speaking to a pair of Macdonald guardsmen. Padraig neared without speaking as his brother instructed the men to split the hours that night, one group sleeping and the second on guard. The men at the seashore had been advised to do the same.

Despite there not seeming to be any threat from the MacLeod, every precaution was to be taken. One never knew.

His brother walked with him to the bedchambers that had been set aside for them. In one Evander would be sleeping, Padraig and Rauri would share the one across the hall.

Once inside Evander's room, he motioned for Padraig to close the door. "He has yet to bring up anything of substance." His brother was clearly annoyed.

"After last meal, ye bring it up," Padraig stated. "Then once we discuss the border issue, we can return."

He gave Evander a pointed look. "Under no circumstances will ye consider any match between me and Iona MacLeod. She is unbearable."

Evander smiled. "I have no desire to be permanently joined with this clan. Did ye know he has a son? From what a guard told Rauri, the son left as soon as he became of age."

"Probably could not stand being around his father."

"Aye, it was after the mother died."

The son would be laird one day. Padraig wondered where the man bided his time until his father's death. "We should try to find the son. Once he becomes laird, it would be beneficial to know what kind of man he is."

"Aye, true," Evander replied.

Upon entering the great room for last meal, Lady MacLeod insisted that Padraig sit at the family table. The laird, his first, and Evander were at the high board. Next to Evander was Rauri.

"Iona will be sitting here alone, it would be nice if ye accompany her," Lady MacLeod said in a soothing voice. "It would be kind of ye."

Iona sat at the table leaning forward, her feline-like eyes locked on him. Padraig shuddered internally.

Just then Iona looked away, her eyes widening. At the same time, Lady MacLeod's expression of surprise made him look to where they did.

A beautiful lass walked into the room. With rich brown waves pulled up to her crown, allowing the rest to fall down her back. She looked a vision. By her blank expression, it was obvious Freya didn't notice how much attention she garnered.

She wore a simple pale green dress that, by contrast to her stepsister's highly embellished one, emphasized how beautiful she was.

As she made her way to the table, her eyes lifted to his and her lips curved in acknowledgment.

"Perhaps yer brother would prefer ye join him on the high board," Lady MacLeod stated. "I can sit with... them."

"Nay,"—Padraig took the woman's elbow and guided her to the high board—"enjoy yer meal."

He then hurried back to the table where Iona and Freya were to sit.

He held out the chair for Freya. "Ye combed yer hair. I like it."

Rolling her eyes playfully, she chuckled. "Ye would be shocked to know that I also bathed."

"I am."

As they bantered, Iona's eyes narrowed. "Ye should not be so familiar with a single man, Freya. 'Tis not becoming."

Ignoring the other woman, Freya reached for the bread. "I am so hungry."

"Ye should not be running about like some sort of street urchin," Iona said. She then looked to Padraig. "Freya insists on acting as if she's not part of the family. The laird's own daughter. 'Tis disgraceful and quite embarrassing. I do hope ye excuse it."

Freya acted as if Iona didn't speak and instead looked to the servant who brought food. "Thank ye Isla."

The servant smiled broadly at Freya, her smile disappearing at Iona's disapproving look.

The meal was good, admittedly better with Freya sitting to his right. Unfortunately, Iona spoke the entire time. With each story she ensured to sprinkle it with unflattering bits about Freya.

"If not for my interference, Freya would have been taken by the traveling gypsies as they thought her one of their own." Iona abruptly stopped yet another diatribe about what a bother Freya was when Freya laughed.

Face bright, Freya looked to Padraig. "I was tempted to go with them. They are a cheerful bunch, who loved music and singing. And whatever they were cooking smelled wonderful."

Padraig barked out laughing, much to the dismay of a fuming Iona.

CHAPTER FOUR

"I HAVE NEVER given the MacLeod's on yer isle instructions to fight over borders. There must be a reason they feel the land is threatened," The MacLeod spoke with a conciliatory tone that made Padraig grind his back molars.

Somehow Evander managed a relaxed demeanor. "What I am asking is for ye to send a messenger to ensure they understand any kind of attacks will not be tolerated."

The MacLeod let out a breath. "Very well. However, I must go there myself. To see where this border is and why there are, as ye put it, so many problems there."

"I said attacks. The death and injury of people are more than just a problem." Evander stood. "I welcome yer visit at any time. My men and I will depart tomorrow."

The MacLeod leaned back, his shrewd gaze taking Evander in. "Yer father was more of a diplomat than ye. He would have stayed at least a pair of days to ensure good comradery between us."

"And was there?" Evander asked. "Ye and father were never friends."

The MacLeod stood. Not a tall man, nowhere near Evander or Padraig's height. However, he made up for his lack in stature with a hard demeanor. "Stay another day. We can travel back together."

Of course Evander had to accept. Otherwise, it would be an insult to their host. "Ye are gracious. I did not wish to overstay our welcome."

The lie seemed to satisfy the MacLeod. "A day or two will not matter in the scheme of things. I must ensure all is in order here, then we can travel to North Uist and see about this prob...situation."

Upon returning to Evander's bedchamber, his brother paced the room. "One day, but no more. Whatever this man is up to, I do not trust him."

"We can send a scout to ensure there isn't something occurring back on Uist," Padraig suggested.

"Good idea," Evander replied. "Go to the shore under the cover of darkness. Send a scout. Tell him to send word back immediately."

"I could go," Padraig offered.

"Nay, yer absence will be questioned." Evander went to the window and peered out. "Hopefully ye can pass through the gates and get to our men without being seen."

His lips curved. "I know of a way in and out without being seen."

Upon returning from his errand, the night was dark, only a half-moon providing feeble light with which to see.

Padraig had already stumbled several times as he rounded the wall, to find the place through which he'd seen Freya return from the village the day before.

Just as he approached the opening, voices made him stop. It was the guards atop the wall, they spoke and chuckled. Obviously nothing serious.

He slipped through the lopsided gate and then remained as close to the stables as he could so to not be seen. Once he arrived at the well, he waited for a moment and then hurried to the back of the house.

Deciding it was best to enter through a different doorway he searched for a back entrance.

There was a door, but to his disappointment it was bolted, so he gave up. If anyone came upon him, he'd use the excuse of being unable to sleep and taking a walk. Hopefully it would not arouse suspicion.

Just then a light caught his eye and Padraig looked past the open window. Inside Freya sat on the floor. In front of her, clothes and other miscellaneous items were neatly folded and stacked. She held out a finger and counted the short stacks and then tapped her chin in thought.

Finally, she stood and brought a satchel over and began to place the items in it. The lass was planning to travel. Was her family aware?

"Freya?" he whispered.

He may as well have shouted by how high she jumped at the sound of his voice.

The lass scrambled to the window with a murderous expression. "Ye just gave me the fright of my life. Why were ye spying through my window?"

Padraig frowned. "I was walking past and saw the light."

Scanning the area behind him, she then met his gaze. "Why are ye out in the middle of the night?"

"I was having trouble sleeping."

At the words, her face brightened. "Come with me to the kitchen. I will boil herbs that will have ye asleep in no time."

"How do I get in?"

Freya bit her bottom lip as she considered his question, it was adorable. Then her lips pursed, and right eyebrow rose. "There is a door to yer left, I will open it." She disappeared and Padraig went back to the one he'd tried earlier.

Moments later, they sat across from each other in the dimly lit kitchen. A cup of steaming liquid before him, Padraig took a tentative sip. Although he could smell herbs, the flavor was nonexistent.

"Ye were packing," Padraig said meeting her gaze. "Traveling somewhere?"

Even in the dimness, the brightness of her cheeks said he'd guessed correctly. Freya shook her head. "I am not. However, I am always prepared for whatever adventure awaits."

"There is nowhere to go that yer father will not find ye. Ye live on a small isle."

When her eyes met his, they were questioning. As if she was gauging whether to trust him or not.

"Why are ye so kind to me?" she asked. "Certainly ye are here to get to know my father, perhaps be matched with Iona…" She let the sentence drift.

Padraig frowned. "Am I to understand that ye find my company bothersome? Ye wound me fair lass."

Although her lips twitched, she didn't outright smile. "Ye avoid the question sir."

"I find yer company refreshing," Padraig stated honestly. "Ye are like no one I've ever met before." He frowned. "I have an idea."

Eyes wide, Freya leaned forward. "If it is a way for me to get away from here, I am all ears."

"First ye must tell me why ye wish to leave."

Freya stood and walked to the doorway as if needing to escape the room if need be. "I have many reasons."

Padraig came up behind her. "There must be a very strong reason for a lass to wish to go out into the world alone. Out there is not a safe place Freya. Not without protection. How would ye survive?"

When she turned, her mouth fell open at realizing how close they were. He almost laughed when she hitched her chin, in an effort to prove that he did not affect her. And he would've thought her unaffected if not for the fast breathing.

"May I?" He leaned closer, unsure why his every instinct urged him to kiss her like he'd wanted to since the first time he'd seen her. However, his head blared a different warning. Kissing Freya was going to be the biggest mistake of his life.

Nevertheless, at her subtle nod, he pressed his lips to hers. Freya shuddered, then placed her hands on his shoulders as if to steady herself.

Tentative at first, he pressed soft kisses across her lips, then deepened the kiss suckling her bottom lip before pulling back.

Her eyes fluttered open, and she stared into his. "That was nice."

"I am glad ye approve of my technique." Padraig wasn't sure what to think. The lass studied him then to his surprise, lifted to her toes and pressed a long kiss to the corner of his lips.

Stepping back, she let out a long breath. "I wish to leave because I am tired of the slaps across my face. To be treated like an outsider in my own home breaks my heart every single day. I have lost my father's affection and other than some of the servants, I rarely receive a kind word. This is no longer my home Padraig. I wish to leave and begin a new life. I'd rather live as a villager, selling herbs than to continue here."

As he listened, Padraig had to agree that since arriving he'd noticed the way Freya was treated. It was more than obvious she was inconsequential to the family.

"Ye can come to North Uist for a visit. Decide what to do from there. Yer father is coming, I will state that ye are coming as my personal guest."

Her face brightened. "Ye will do that for me?"

"Of course," Padraig said, then considered he'd have to make up a reason for his request. He met her gaze. "I will have to tell him—"

"Who's there?" A woman walked into the kitchen holding up a candle. "Lass…" she began before noticing Padraig. "Sir, do ye require something?"

"I boiled some herbs for him so that he can sleep," Freya said with a wide smile. "Come Eva, let us make our way back to our beds." With a quick look of gratitude over her shoulder to him, she and the cook walked away, down the darkened corridor.

HER SMALL BEDCHAMBER suddenly seemed to take on a life of its own when Freya entered. The clothes she'd folded remained on her bed, the curtains blew inward as she'd left the window open after hurrying off to let Padraig in.

The breeze caused the candlelight to flicker casting dancing shadows against the walls. She looked at her reflection in the small handheld mirror that had been her mother's. Her eyes were dark, cheeks flushed. The hollowness she'd been accustomed to seeing in her gaze was gone. In its place, there was a glimmer. It was hope she finally had an ally, someone who saw the truth of her situation and was willing to help.

Why had he kissed her? The action had both startled and delighted her. It had felt natural, as if a kiss between them was inevitable. Her lips curved. She'd dared to kiss him back. Mostly because after one kiss, she'd wanted more. Padraig probably found her childish, but it had been the most adult thing she'd ever done with a man.

Her heart threatened to break out of her chest as Freya considered what would happen. Was she truly prepared to start a new life? A life that took her away from everything familiar.

If she had her way, she would prefer to live in the nearby village, surrounded by people she'd grown to care for. However, her father would never approve of his daughter doing so. Not that he cared about her, it was his reputation that would lead him to deny her request to live elsewhere.

She'd hinted at it before. Had asked for a cottage on the edge of the village. Her father had become angry and sent her away. "Do not be ungrateful for what ye have."

In truth, Freya had to admit, she did have food and shelter and if she asked her father, he would probably give her coin for new clothes and shoes. Perhaps she was being rash. She could ask to be married off. It would be a way out. Marriage would bring a home and family of her own. After all, that is what she wished for more than anything.

Walking over to the bed she fell upon it, ignoring the folded clothes.

"WHAT ARE YE doing?" Orla stood just outside the kitchen doorway, as if entering would soil her in some way. Her sharp eyes scanned over Freya with disapproval. "Go and change immediately."

Freya wore a simple frock that she felt was appropriate for visitors. Or so she thought.

She was hoping to save the other new one for when she traveled. However, now that she'd realized to be too nervous to go through with it, it didn't matter Freya supposed.

When she walked closer, Orla took her arm in a painful grip. "Stay away from him. If anyone is to get Padraig Macdonald's attention, it will be Iona."

"Ye are hurting me," Freya said between winces. "Stop it."

Thankfully the woman released her arm and sneered. "On second thought, do not change. Remain as unremarkable as ye prefer. Make yerself useful and help Iona dress." She walked away.

Freya blew out a breath and turned on her heel. The last thing she wanted was Iona's company that morning. Besides, she had a more pressing issue. To find Padraig and inform him she'd changed her mind. It was best to get it over with. Accept her fate, remain there, and pray that her father find her an unremarkable husband. Someone who would not be too old or mistreat her.

Her stepmother disappeared down the corridor and Freya returned to the kitchen.

"Eva, I think today would be a good day to remain in my room." She grinned at the cook, who shook her head.

"First I suggest a walk in the garden. Some of yer herbs require watering and clipping."

"Good idea," Freya replied. "That will be another good place to not be bothered by them."

Just then a servant girl entered and rushed to her. "Miss Freya, yer father requests yer presence in the great room."

She and Eva exchanged confused looks. Freya let out a sigh. "Orla must have complained about me."

Walking into the great room, she froze at the venomous glare her stepmother directed at her before turning to her father. He sat with both Laird Macdonald and Padraig. Everyone turned to look at her with varying expressions.

Her father studied her with curiosity, as if noticing things about her for the first time he'd not seen before.

"Come here lass," her father instructed, motioning with his right hand. Although his gaze remained curious, his expression did soften upon her nearing.

"We are to all go visit with the Macdonald's in North Uist. Padraig has insisted ye come as his guest."

Her breath caught and her eyes rounded. First, she looked to Padraig, who seemed to be fighting to keep from laughing at her expression. Next, she met the Macdonald's gaze. He didn't seem to find the situation humorous at all. Instead he studied her with a slight frown.

Finally, when she let out her breath in a loud whoosh, she met her father's gaze. "I am honored," she finally managed, lowering her gaze to the floor.

Whatever Padraig was up to, it would not work. She'd changed her mind realizing that she had nowhere to go. Her mother had a sister on Rona, a small Isle off the coast of Skye, but she'd not seen them since her mother's death.

Then again, a long visit on another isle giving her more time to get her thoughts together would be pleasant. Especially if it meant getting away from Orla and Iona for a fortnight.

CHAPTER FIVE

THE TRIP TO North Uist was normally a quiet interlude. The birlinn's movements slow and steady. Giving one time to think and take in the beauty of the surroundings as the vessels sliced their way through the sea waters.

Padraig looked to the other vessel that held his and Evander's steeds. The huge brave animals stood stock-still, as if instinctively knowing any rash movements meant the possibility of overturning the oversized boats.

"As ye can see, it is imperative that people like us remain allies to keep enemies at bay. There are dangers everywhere, even in our own homes." The MacLeod had not stopped boasting since they'd set off on horseback to the birlinns.

Padraig had expected the man would sail on his own vessels, but instead had insisted it was a perfect time for them to finally discuss everything he'd not made time for while at the keep. It made Padraig wonder if the man indeed did have enemies in his own home.

Evander spoke next. "I agree that being allied is to the benefit of both clans. However, the people must be informed and kept in line. No matter what we do as lairds, people have minds of their own and have to be reminded of our mandates."

The MacLeod waved his hand dismissively. "I do not concern myself overly with those on Harris. However, I do admit those that remain on North Uist are a bother."

"Ye can appoint a man to be yer representative at the village," Padraig suggested.

"When ye do that, they start to plot how to take what is rightfully yers away," the MacLeod replied giving Padraig a narrow-eyed look. "Ye should consider it before deciding to appoint anyone to yer tasks.

Padraig fought not to roll his eyes at the annoying man. Instead, he looked behind to the MacLeod's birlinn, upon which were Freya, Lady MacLeod, and Iona, who had insisted on going as well. He spied Freya standing at the front of the vessel looking out across the water, her face bright with excitement.

Upon noticing him, she waved at him in acknowledgement. He couldn't help but to smile back lifting his hand in return.

At the clearing of Evander's throat, Padraig turned to his brother who lifted an eyebrow in amusement. A glance to Freya's father, who was now talking about punishing guards on North Uist, told he'd not noticed the exchange between himself and Freya.

Upon arriving at his home, Padraig held back at the gates to wait for Freya.

Seeming to forget his daughter was in tow, the MacLeod had walked into the keep with his wife and Iona, who kept glancing at him, as if expecting Padraig to come inside with them.

Lady MacLeod and Iona had insisted there wasn't room in

their carriage for Freya after their companions climbed in. So Freya had accepted the offer of one of their guards to ride to the keep on the front seat of a wagon.

Unbeknownst to her stepmother and Iona, Freya had the best view of the surroundings and could take in the entire keep without the impediment of the carriage. He rode alongside watching her as she'd taken in his home, her eyes widening at the appearance of the white-stoned beauty that stood proudly atop a rising.

She grinned at him, letting him know she found his home stunning.

They did not exchange many words as guards remained close, both MacLeod and Macdonald.

Not allowing another person near, Padraig assisted Freya from the wagon, placing both hands at her waist and lowering her to the ground. Her cheeks pinkened at the nearness between them, but she managed to compose herself quickly.

"Yer home is beautiful," she gushed, looking around the large courtyard. "So well kept. I cannot wait to see the inside."

He turned to find that his mother and Ella stood at the front door to greet them. Obviously, Evander had informed them there was another family member to arrive.

They greeted Freya warmly, the lass seeming a bit overwhelmed by the look of confusion on her face.

"Welcome Freya," Ella said holding Freya's hands in her own. "I look forward to getting to know ye. I am so glad ye plan to stay."

"I agree with Ella," his mother added. "It is always a treat to have female company." The women ushered Freya in, leaving him to follow.

The MacLeod sat at the family table, a guard to his right and Evander to his left. On Evander's left sat Rauri, who gave him a dull look. Evidently everyone was already tiring of the MacLeod's nonstop dialog.

Servants rushed out from the kitchens with trays laden with bowls of steaming stew, others with platters of breads. While cups were filled with ale, the visitors were treated to a meal of stew, cheese, and roasted vegetables from the gardens.

His mother, his sister-in-law, along with Freya joined the MacLeod's wife and Iona at a table close to the laird's table. Padraig lingered a bit before joining Evander's table, resigned to an evening that would no doubt prove to be long.

AFTER THE MEAL, he, Evander, and the MacLeod went to the parlor where they joined the ladies. His mother and Ella had set up honeyed mead in glasses as well as fruit tarts for the visitors.

The MacLeod had talked the entire meal about inconsequential things and had apparently tired himself out because only moments after sitting in the comfortable overstuffed chair in the parlor, he fell asleep.

Lady MacLeod gave her husband an annoyed look before turning her attention to Padraig's mother. "Lady Aileen, yer eldest made a remarkable match with Lady Ella. Ye must advise me in how to do the same with my beautiful Iona."

His mother's lips curved into what he knew to be her polite smile. "Of course. Although I am sure there are plenty of suitors to choose from." After a slight hesitation, his mother's gaze sliding to a very still Freya, she added. "What of Freya? Is she spoken for?"

"Oh, no, it will be hard to find her a suitor with her… ways." The woman huffed and looked up at the ceiling. "My husband's first wife did not take the time to take her in hand. Did she Freya?" She gave Freya a sharp look.

Padraig looked away from his conversation with Evander and Rauri to listen.

"My mother taught me well for my first seven years. I owe the fact I can read, write, and understand numbers to her. She also taught me to embroider, catch fish, and simple cookery. I have lived with ye for the last twelve, I do not recall even one lesson. Ye were otherwise occupied, I suppose."

Evander coughed to cover a chuckle. Ella on the other hand could barely hide her giggle.

"Impertinent," Lady MacLeod said with a huff. "Ye sat in on Iona's many lessons."

Freya's silence told the woman lied.

Annoyed at not being the center of attention Iona let out a breathy, "Goodness, it is a beautiful view. I wonder if it would be possible to be escorted outside for a walk?"

At Padraig's slight shake of his head, Ella smiled widely and stood. "What a delightful idea. Let us go for a walk. Join us Freya."

Iona's smiled tightened, her eyes shifting to Padraig who turned to Evander. "Can we speak?"

"I will remain here with Lady MacLeod," his mother stated. "Ye should try these delightful tarts. We pride ourselves in our cook, Willa's, mastery in the kitchen."

As shadows fell across the garden from the setting sun, Freya took in the surroundings. It was a picturesque place where the keep was located. Over the garden's short wall, she could see past the taller surrounding keep wall to the seashore. There the birlinns bobbed in the water, men walked around a bonfire where they would spend the night.

A village to the far right came into view just past trees where she imagined people did whatever they had to as the day ended, and their evening routines would begin.

She tracked a lone man on a wagon being pulled by a mule, who seemed more interested in stopping every so often to nibble on grasses than to get his master to their destination.

The man finally snapped the reins only to be rewarded by the animal kicking its back legs and almost overturning the wagon. Freya giggled and pointed to the wagon.

Ella followed her line of sight. "Ah, yes, that is old man Hugo and his stubborn mule, Renata. He refuses to get rid of the beast despite the fact he is always complaining about how slow she is. They are a colorful duo."

They watched the man's progress for a bit before Iona joined them. "Is Padraig courting anyone?"

Her abrupt question made Ella turn to her sharply. "I believe he is interested in someone here. It has been decided Padraig is free to choose who to marry. He will not be matched."

"I see," Iona replied, her sharp gaze taking Ella in. "What of ye? Were ye matched?"

"No," Ella replied. "Why don't I show ye the house."

Freya enjoyed the tour of the house, especially meeting, Willa, the family cook. The woman was probably in her late twenties, quite young to be head cook. She had an honest and open personality and immediately described to them what they would be served to break their fast in the morning. With hair pulled tightly away from her round pretty face, her bright blue eyes met Freya's for only an instant before she offered to bring warmed cider to the parlor.

"That would be wonderful," Ella said. "We shall go there momentarily once I show our guests where their bedchambers are."

"WHAT IS ON yer mind?" Evander asked as they sat back in his brother's study. "Why did ye insist on the lass Freya coming along?"

He ignored his brother's attempt at a knowing look. "I like her company. She is intelligent and not at all like the rest of them. If we are to endure the MacLeod, I thought it good to have an agreeable distraction."

"She probably would not have been included." Evander's statement surprised him. Obviously his brother had noticed how differently Freya was treated. "Be careful that the lass does not expect something from ye because ye personally invited her."

"She is not like that," Padraig replied. "Freya is unlike most women I have met."

Evander shrugged. "We must not allow the MacLeod to attempt any distractions. I am considering going with him to the borderlands. That he brought so many men with him is worrisome."

"Aye, I am glad ye insisted that most come and stay here in the keep courtyard. Better to keep an eye on them."

His brother looked to the doorway to ensure no one listened. "Were the men instructed to keep an eye on those out by the bìrlinns?"

"Aye," Padraig said. "Rauri is gone now to ensure there are no stragglers that could be trying to sneak away to the borderlands."

"We must stay vigilant. I do not trust him," Evander stated his gaze flat. "There is something he is not saying. Either he brings so many because he is up to no good, or he is afraid of what awaits him at the border."

"I wondered the same," Padraig replied. "I get the feeling the large contingency is because he has not been in contact with the people here and they no longer consider themselves part of their clan."

Evander leaned forward. "If they do not, we will not engage. Instead, we will allow them to fight their own battle. I will not put our men at risk for his lack of diligence."

"How many men should ye take?" Padraig became worried. "Perhaps we should rethink things. Instead of us going with him tomorrow, we should send a contingency to look on, but remain at a distance."

His brother considered what he said. "Aye, I agree. Let us make an excuse. Ye and I will have an urgent matter to see to tomorrow and will leave at dawn. From what I gathered while we were in Harris, the MacLeod is a late sleeper."

"I feel better. The last thing we need is to be involved in turmoil within a clan. Especially when one half lives here closer to us."

Suddenly Evander's lips pressed together. "I think that is why he asked that I come to Harris and then returned with us. He wishes for the people who live north of us to think we are his allies and will fight alongside him. The man has no idea what awaits him and plans to use us as a deterrent."

CHAPTER SIX

It was early morning when Freya woke a bit confused. Just the air coming through the window that she'd left cracked smelled different. There was a sweet fragrance in the air from the garden below.

She'd been shocked by the beautiful bedroom she'd been given. Of course, the Macdonalds considered her station as the laird's only daughter.

It made her wonder what her life would have been like if her mother had lived. Beautiful bedchambers, plush beddings, and servants at her disposal. Instead, she'd been slowly moved farther away from where her father, Orla, and Iona slept.

First with excuses of needing her bedchamber for visitors, then Orla making excuses as to why she did not require such a large room.

Admittedly, none of the bedchambers back home were as plush and exquisitely decorated as the one she currently slept in. Beautifully embroidered tapestries on the walls, thick blankets and downy soft pillows on the bed, all made for an inviting space.

The furniture was dark wood, intricately carved with patterns of leaves and flowers. Both the headboard and dressing table seemed to have been crafted by the same person.

From what she remembered, her mother had enjoyed

decorating, Orla not so much. Her embroidery was gaudy at best and neither she nor Iona seemed to ever finish a project before moving to the next.

As for Freya, she had embroidered a few tapestries, which she hung in her bedroom, but as of late she's spent all her free time concentrating on gardening and harvesting herbs.

Again she took in the room and decided that upon returning home, she'd not ask permission, but instead move to a larger space and redecorate it. Even if she'd not remain long as she was sure to be married off soon, there was no need to allow for the disrespect she received to continue.

It had to stop.

At a knock on the door, she sat up. "Come in."

A young chambermaid entered with a tray. "Willa sends ye some hot cider and biscuits. Ye told her ye woke up very early and first meal will not be for another pair of hours."

Freya's eyes widened. "She is magical." She was in awe at the fact the young cook would remember her comment.

"Aye, she is," the maid replied with a smile. Once placing the tray down, she looked to Freya. "Would ye like a bath brought?"

"I very much would." Freya practically danced across the room to where the cup of cider awaited. "This will be a very enjoyable visit," she said out loud.

THE BATH WAS indulgent. The hot fragrant water lulled her eyes closed as she sunk deeper into the wooden tub that had been brought to her room and filled by two lads. Along with the tub she had been given oil for her skin and thick cloths to dry with.

If guests were treated this well, it would be hard to return to her humdrum life afterwards.

There was a quick rap on the door and Freya called out for them to enter expecting a servant was returning to see if she was finished. As long as the water retained warmth, she would refuse to get out of the tub.

At the door opening and closing, she kept her eyes closed. "A few more minutes. The water is still very warm, and I have yet to wash my hair."

At the clearing of a male throat, Freya sat up straight and her eyes flew open. His back to her, Padraig glanced over his shoulder, just long enough to see her bared breasts. Gasping, she crossed her arms over her chest and sunk back into the water.

"What are ye doing here? Ye should not have entered."

"Ye said to come in," he replied in a jovial tone while keeping his back to her. "I came to tell ye that I will be gone until after late morning."

If it was possible to feel more exposed, Freya could not grasp how. "Aye, fine, just please go."

The man had the nerve to chuckle. "I am glad ye are enjoying the bath I suggested it be brought. I have a few more surprises in store for ye today."

"Go!" she repeated. "This is most inappropriate. Someone may see ye leave my bedchamber."

"No one other than my brother is awake."

When he began to turn, Freya sunk down to her chin, doing her best to cover herself with her arms and hands.

Padraig met her gaze, his eyes not moving away. "I am glad ye are here pretty lass." With that he walked to the door and left.

Letting out a long breath, Freya stared at the closed door. Padraig Macdonald was the most interesting man she'd ever met. And he was also the most handsome.

Moments later, she sat drying her hair by the window, allowing the breeze to blow through it as she finger combed out the tangles. In a few moments she'd go to the kitchens and see about helping. Idle time did not agree with her, and she did not wish to disturb the household by meandering about.

Perhaps she would get to spend more time with Ella Macdonald. The laird's wife—who was perhaps a year or two older than her—was nice and Freya wished to get to know her better.

Just as she finished braiding her hair, the same chambermaid returned with two lads who dispatched with the bathwater and tub in short order. The maid picked up the used drying cloths and looked to the door, where a second maid entered with a blue gown over her arms and matching ribbons in her hands.

"A gift from Master Padraig," the maid stated. "He said to tell ye it is a gift from his family for ye." The maid smiled brightly. "I can help ye dress."

It was strange to be assisted to dress. Although, with the intricate ties and layers, she would have had trouble dressing herself. Once the dress was on, the maid weaved ribbons into her hair and then wrapped the braids around her hair like a sort of crown.

Freya had never worn her hair this way, it felt different. As if she'd donned a hat.

"Ye look lovely miss," the maid said holding up a hand

mirror. "Most bonnie."

The person looking back could not possibly be her. Bright green eyes and a flushed face complemented by the hairstyle and square collar of the gown made her look like someone of importance.

Freya giggled. "I feel as if playing dress up." She took the maid's hand. "Thank ye very much. Can ye tell me who this dress belonged to?"

"Our laird's sister, Beatrice, had so many gowns that she could not take them all upon marrying a Ross. She now lives in South Uist and no longer wants them. Mistress Beatrice instructed that if ever a lass came that could use them, they would be her gift. A few have been given to anyone who visits that is small enough, which is rare."

Freya smiled. "This one is beautiful."

"I am glad ye like it because Master Padraig has instructed that we bring ye a different one tomorrow. He said to tell ye they are all yers to have."

"Orla and Iona will definitely not like this," Freya whispered when the maid left. A part of her was delighted, but a fear of what Orla and Iona would do to make her feel badly about wearing clothes that did not belong to her was worrying.

Freya shrugged. She didn't care if they said it. Just this one gown was more beautiful than anything Iona owned. They would not fit her since Iona was much taller and had larger breasts.

With a bright smile, she left the bedchamber and strolled down a corridor. There was a landing from which she could look down into the great room. Freya hesitated to take in the large space below.

She could not remember in which direction the kitchens were. Upon spying a pair of maids entering and preparing the room for first meal, she hurried to the stairwell.

"What are ye doing?" Freya whirled around to find a very astounded Iona. Strange that she was up and dressed. Iona normally had to be roused from sleep in the mornings. Eyes traveling from Freya's hair to her slippered feet, Iona finished by meeting her gaze with a rounded one.

"Where did ye get those clothes? Mother will be displeased. I am sure ye stole them."

"I did not steal them. They were a gift."

Eyes narrowed and face scrunched up, Iona looked like a rabid squirrel. "Ye are a liar. No one gave ye those clothes." She neared, lifting a hand. The slap surprised Freya and she stumbled back, almost falling down the stairs. Thankfully she managed to grab the railing.

"Remove those clothes at once," Iona hissed.

"Get away from me," Freya replied doing her best to push past Iona, who moved to block her from going down the stairs.

When Freya tried to get past, Iona grabbed her hair and pulled it so hard, Freya fell backward to the floor.

Suddenly, Iona shrieked and covered her face with both hands. "I cannot believe ye hit me."

"Wh-what?" Freya stuttered.

Both Macdonald women hurried toward them.

Freya tried to get to her feet, but she stepped on the gown's hem making her look like an awkward idiot. Finally she stood and looked to Iona, who managed to spill a pair of tears.

"She is the worst sister. Hit me for no reason other than asking if she stole that dress." Iona could barely keep up the pretense, her eyes turning to slits upon looking toward Freya.

Not waiting to hear anymore, Freya turned on her heel and rushed back to the bedchamber and took off the gown.

Moments later, she was back in her plain dress sitting by the window, her gaze fixed out, but not seeing anything.

No one came to invite her to first meal, which was the norm. Thankfully she'd eaten the bit the servants had brought earlier. When her stomach growled, she swallowed a sob. Her life was never going to change. Why did she dare think it would?

It was sometime later that there was a knock on the door and upon her calling out, the same servant who'd dressed and combed her hair entered. Her gaze took Freya in for a few beats before speaking.

"Lady Ella wishes to speak to ye. She is in the sitting room."

"Of course," Freya said standing. If they asked that she stay in her bedchamber or return to Harris, she would accept it without argument. Perhaps it would be the perfect time to escape. While everyone was here.

"Follow me."

The sitting room was on the second floor, down the corridor from where Freya slept. When she entered, Freya was surprised to find that Orla and Iona as well as Laird Macdonald's mother were there.

Iona gave her a triumphant look.

Her heart threatened to burst out of her chest. Freya absently reached up to her head. She'd not bothered to fix the lopsided hairdo and in all probability she looked ridiculous.

"I must address this," Ella began, her expression unreadable. "Mother and I are astonished at what we witnessed this morning."

Freya didn't dare look up, instead kept her gaze on her folded hands. It was all she could do not to die of embarrassment that Padraig's family think her so vulgar as to fight with Iona unprovoked.

"I must apologize," Orla began. "We tried to dissuade yer son from inviting her—"

"May I speak?" Ella interrupted in a firm tone.

Freya could not help but look to see Orla's astonished expression that was soon replaced with barely hidden annoyance.

"What we saw," Ella continued, "was Iona assaulting Freya, both verbally and physically. She accused her of stealing the dress Padraig gifted her, and then slapped her so hard she stumbled. Ye can still see the mark on her face."

Iona gasped. "Ye must have not seen what happened before that. It was she who assaulted me."

Lady Aileen gave Iona an incredulous look. "I was standing in the corridor admiring how lovely the gown looked on Freya before ye walked out of yer bedchamber. It was ye who provoked what happened. As a matter of fact, I did not see Freya do more than protect herself. This is horrifying behavior," she finished looking to Orla whose face was beet red.

"How dare ye," Iona's ready stream of tears slid down her face. She stood and stared at the laird's mother. "I was simply worried that she'd taken from yer home without permission."

The room was silent as it seemed neither of the Macdonald women were sure how to respond to yet another lie.

"I should not have worn the gown," Freya stated. "It was

kind of yer family to offer it, however, I should have asked permission before donning the clothes."

"It was thoughtless of ye Freya," Orla said sitting up straighter. "Obviously it was a misunderstanding. Freya go to yer bedchamber and remain there until we leave."

Ella and her mother-in-law exchanged confused looks at the fact she was to be punished despite doing nothing wrong. However, since it was not their place to correct what happened, they refrained from speaking.

Embarrassed and feeling lower than she'd ever felt, Freya stood and rushed from the room a sob caught in her throat.

In the corridor, Padraig was stepping onto the landing.

"I must remain in my room until we leave," she told him as she hurried past unable to stand the idea that he'd see her in such a state.

She wasn't in the room long before hard knocks made her jump. She stared at the door wishing she'd locked it. If it was Padraig, she would ask him to leave.

"Freya?" His deep voice resonated through the door and straight into her chest. "What happened?"

Wiping away an angry tear, she went to the door and cracked it open. "It is that I do not feel well at all."

His eyes pinned the side of her face Iona had slapped. "Did someone strike ye?"

"I-I bumped into something. Please, I must rest. Perhaps we can go to the village another day." She tried to close the door, but his booted foot prevented it.

"They mistreat ye. Was it the fact ye wore the gown?"

"I should have sought permission from Orla before wearing it. It was my mistake. My head is pounding. Please go."

After a lingering look, finally Padraig backed away from the door allowing her to close it.

WHEN HEADING BACK toward the stairwell, Ella called out Padraig's name. She remained in the sitting room alone. Her hazel gaze met his for a moment. "How is she? Poor lass."

"She claims to have a headache and not feel well." He walked further into the room. "What occurred?"

Ella frowned. "The sister, Iona, hit her and accused her of stealing the gown. Yer mother and I saw the entire exchange. Then Iona tried to pull the ribbons from her hair. Freya did not do more than protect herself. I am sure that if we had not happened upon it, the poor lass would have been pushed down the stairs."

Something in his stomach clenched. "Aye, both the stepmother and stepsister mistreat her regularly. It angers me that the MacLeod does little if anything at all to protect his daughter."

"Perhaps ye should speak to Evander or directly to that horrible man," Ella stated. "I feel terrible for her."

He nodded and left the room. It was not in the nature of men to discuss what happened between females in the household. Whatever happened between women, was usually dealt with by the matriarchs. However, in this case, he felt as if he had to do something.

Upon ascending to the first floor, he noted the front doors were open. Through them, clouds of dust rose as horsemen entered the courtyard.

The MacLeod had returned.

Evander had sent a few Macdonald guardsmen, including Rauri, who'd been instructed to ensure their clan was not pulled into whatever issues came about. Rauri was instructed to ask for a stop to the attacks, even if temporary.

As Padraig neared the front door, Evander exited behind him.

It was more than apparent that the MacLeod was not happy. He growled a greeting, shaking his head as if disappointed in them.

When his brother's gaze met Padraig's, he tried not to laugh. Somehow Evander had managed to say—*he can go to hell*—without speaking a single word.

"Whisky," the MacLeod said upon entering the great room. Evander motioned to a servant to bring beverages as they made their way to a table near the fireplace where they sat. Rauri entered and joined them.

"What happened?" Evander asked although both he and Padraig would find out more once they spoke to Rauri.

The MacLeod waved a hand dismissively, then upon the whisky being served, drank it all down and proffered his cup for a refill.

"It would have been preferable if ye would have traveled with me as we'd discussed." He hesitated as if waiting for Evander to apologize. When it was not forthcoming, he continued, "They have ideas of splitting off from the clan. They've appointed a leader." The MacLeod took another long swig, droplets dribbling down his beard. "Idiots."

The MacLeod looked to Evander for a moment and then scanned the room. "Have any of them approached ye about it?"

The question made his brother clear his throat. Padraig wondered if it was a curse that Evander swallowed. "Nay. As I have told ye. They are very proprietary of the borderlands and thus why I came to speak to ye. That they wish to split and become their own clan could explain why."

"I will not allow it." The MacLeod refilled his own cup this time. "If it is a war they wish, then I will kill every single one of them."

The people on the northern lands had a location that would be easy to defend. With a rocky shoreline behind and steep hills to the front, it wouldn't be difficult to keep attackers at bay. Although not sure of the exact number, there were a few hundred who lived there. The MacLeod would have to bring his entire guard force in order to have a chance of defeating them.

Padraig looked to the man. "If they have made their intentions clear, it is doubtful they will concede. The location of the village, as ye may have discovered will be hard to overtake."

"They've built a keep," the MacLeod hissed. "A damn keep. Who do they think they are?"

His face contorted with rage. "Ye must help me Macdonald. With yer army, it will be easy to defeat them."

"All I wish for is a truce. I can negotiate that on my own," Evander replied. "I will not take my men to war over a few rocky hills. I advise ye give—"

The MacLeod stood. "I see. Then we are not to be allied?" He looked around to ensure no one overheard. "At least give me yer word that ye will not assist them then?"

"I will not help them," Evander responded.

"I wish to believe it." The man suddenly looked defeated. "If my people find out that the village here was allowed to split, they will get ideas." He ran his hand down his beard.

Evander let out a breath. "Ye and I will remain on friendly terms. I have no plans to overtake the people here unless they overstep."

"What guarantee do I have?" The man was despondent, so Evander allowed the insult of the MacLeod not taking him at his word.

Padraig looked to Evander. "It can appear that we are allied. I wish to be handfasted to Freya."

Only he noticed that Evander tensed. However, his brother was good at keeping his feelings hidden.

The MacLeod was nodding even before Padraig and Evander began to negotiate. The handfast did not mean they'd go to battle, but only a reassurance they would remain on friendly terms.

"The lass will remain here," Padraig continued, "It has come to our attention that she is being mistreated." He went on to tell the MacLeod about the morning's occurrence.

WHEN SOMEONE KNOCKED on the door, Freya steeled herself for the next chastisement. It had to be Orla, or perhaps she and Iona had complained to her father, and he came to reprimand her. Too tired to call out, she went to the door and pulled it open.

It was one of her father's guards who gave her a once over and then motioned for her to come with him. "Yer presence is required miss."

"One moment." Freya hurried to the dressing table and after pulling the ribbons from her hair, she brushed it quickly. Then she took her hair with both hands and expertly wrapped it into a bun at the nape of her neck. After, she took one of the ribbons that Padraig had gifted her and tied the hair in place. Perhaps a bit of rebellion was left in her.

The guard didn't seem bothered by having to wait. Instead he nodded as if approving her choice of hairstyle.

"Where are we going?" Freya asked as they made their way down to the first level. Her stomach tumbled at noticing the great room was empty.

"The parlor," he replied taking the familiar path.

Freya touched his arm. "Give me a moment."

Seeming to understand, he stopped and waited as she took several deep breaths. "I feel as if going to my own execution. Except, perhaps being beheaded would be less painful." She frowned in the direction of the parlor.

To her surprise the guard's lips curved. "Family can be like that at times."

"Aye. It is best I face whatever awaits."

In the parlor sat her father, Orla, and Iona. They watched in silence as she walked in.

Iona immediately scanned her outfit, her eyebrows lifting in surprise at seeing she'd donned an older dress.

"There has been a development that we should discuss," her father said. "While I was gone to deal with a pressing situation, facing danger and possible death, embarrassing behavior was taking place here."

Freya let out a breath, whatever her father threw her way

did not matter at this point. He'd probably admonish Iona for slapping her and then both Orla and Iona would take it out on her for days, if not weeks after.

"I have turned a blind eye to what has been occurring for too long. This is my fault for not ensuring that ye show kindness to my daughter," her father said looking at Orla.

The chair Freya sat in seemed to wrap around her, as the surreal scene took place in front of her.

"That Iona slapped her in front of the Macdonald's mother and wife, goes to show how far yer lack of care for her has gone," her father continued.

Freya attempted to decipher if there was any genuine care from her father but could not quite grasp that there was.

Orla attempted to say something, her mouth opening, but her father's sharp look made her stop.

He looked down his nose at his wife and let out a long breath. "As Laird, I must ensure our family is looked upon with admiration, not disdain. Therefore, I have decided that it would be best if Freya no longer lived with us in Harris, where she is constantly subjected to such treatment. I have decided to give her away, in marriage."

Iona's lips curved, a triumphant gleam as she met Freya's eyes. "Fergus Mackinlay will finally get his wish," she said with a shrill giggle. "Congratulations." Her wide grin was most disturbing, and Freya frowned at her.

At the mention of the man who'd come to the Macdonald keep and asked for a wife earlier in the season, Freya shuddered inwardly. Fergus had been widowed, his wife dying in childbirth. He was a distant relative who spent more of his time in the great room at the keep talking to anyone who would listen than he did doing anything else.

The man rarely went home, often spending entire weeks at the keep bemoaning his lack of wife and company. Despite his annoying personality, he was a master craftsman, who produced most of the swords the MacLeod guards used.

Her father studied Iona. "It is ye who will be marrying Mackinlay. A match with him would ensure he does not leave and will continue to produce swords for me."

The air seemed to leave the room as both Orla and Iona gasped loudly. Then Iona fell into her mother's arms sobbing. "No. No. No."

Freya tried to feel badly for her, but Iona would no doubt rule over the poor man, and both would end up living at the keep. Iona's life would barely change.

"About ye, daughter," her father said, capturing Freya's attention. "Ye will remain here as the handfasting ceremony will be done later this day."

"To whom is she to be handfasted to?" Iona stopped sobbing, curiosity being a stronger force.

"Padraig Macdonald has asked for her hand." Her father stood. "Now Freya, go see about wearing something more presentable. We will be celebrating in short order."

Freya refused to meet Iona or Orla's eyes, not sure if what occurred was some type of elaborate prank. Instead she stood and forced her wobbly legs toward the door.

CHAPTER SEVEN

"Have ye lost yer mind?" Evander repeated, his gaze glued to Padraig. Their mother and Ella sat together in a wide chair and looked on, both with similar looks of astonishment at the announcement.

"Son, I would never tell ye what to do," his mother began. "However, in this instance, I beg of ye to reconsider. Despite the fact that Evander does not guarantee an alliance with Clan MacLeod, if ye marry the lass our clan will still be bound to theirs forever."

Padraig stood, went to the door, and closed it. He leaned on it and looked to his family. "I do not plan to marry the lass. She wishes to be free. To go away. After the MacLeod's return to Harris, I will ensure her safe travel to wherever she wishes. I believe her mother has relatives on the coast of Scotland or thereabouts."

Evander looked to the ceiling. "Ye will be held responsible for her disappearing. I will not allow it."

"Whether ye allow it or not, it will happen. I cannot continue to stand by as every member of that family mistreats Freya. Ye must agree with me that it is distressing to see and know that we are not doing something for the lass."

His mother shook her head. "Evander has spoken to her father, and he promised to set his wife and stepdaughter straight on the matter. It is not right for us to interfere. What if the lass ends up in a similar or worse situation with people she barely knows? What then?"

The question made Padraig falter. He'd not considered it.

"It is only a handfasting. After a short period, she can return to Harris, and perhaps she will be offered a better life," Ella said. "Or, in the meantime, we can work on perhaps finding her a proper husband to ask for her hand in marriage, since ye seem reluctant to. Though I know ye are attracted to her."

Evander's lips quivered. "Mother, I am not worried about the MacLeod. He is a weak leader." He then looked to Padraig. "Ye should just marry her and get this over with. She cannot possibly be sent off to whatever awaits."

Feeling woefully unprepared for the consequences of his request to handfast, Padraig shrugged. "I will consider everything ye have stated. I will not send her away but will work with Ella to find her a proper husband."

His mother blew out a breath. "Meanwhile we must suffer the MacLeod and that awful woman, Orla, for who knows how much longer."

"The daughter is not much better," he added.

WHEN PADRAIG WALKED out of the sitting room, he was yanked into a doorway and was surprised to find it was Freya who stood there.

Freya glared up at him. "What do ye think to be doing? Yer going to be tied to my family if the handfasting takes place. I know ye do not wish that."

Echoing what his family had just said, it was as if everyone thought the same thing.

Standing so close to her made Padraig instantly aware that Ella was right, he was attracted to the beauty.

Her darkened green eyes took him in. "Well?"

"I have a plan," he began, then stopped. If he told her the truth, she would refuse to be handfasted. Instead, he wrapped his arms around her waist and pulled her against him.

Her wide eyes moved to his mouth, and it was all the invitation he required. At once his mouth covered hers. Need surged and Padraig deepened the kiss. Her lips were soft and pillowy, her curvy body luscious against his more muscular one. She smelled of herbs and sweetness, a scent he now recognized as hers.

When she finally relaxed against him, giving herself fully to the kiss, Padraig's entire body became engulfed with need. He wanted her, there was no arguing that fact. However, he would not spoil her. Freya deserved restraint and respect.

Her soft moan brought him back to the moment. He slid both hands down her sides and gently pushed her back before breaking the kiss. "We are to be handfasted because ye deserve a better life." Padraig decided to leave it at that.

Freya however would not hear of it. "It is not yer responsibility to look after me. If ye wish to have me for a wife—which I doubt—then I will accept. Otherwise, please do not do this."

Unable to think of what else to say, he pressed a kiss to the tip of her nose. "I will see ye at the ceremony." With that he strode off, his gait much more assured than he felt.

The handfasting was to take place in the family chapel that evening. In the meanwhile, Padraig decided to pass the time at swordplay. He'd planned to take Freya to the village, but now it would have to wait until the next day.

As he walked out, Padraig scratched his head. Handfasting did not require any type of consummation. Would her father insist she be moved into his bedchamber?

Needing air, he decided to go in search of his mother who usually spent the afternoons in her garden.

Upon spotting her in among the plants with Lady MacLeod and a somber looking Iona, he slipped into the back of the house to avoid being seen.

"What can I do for ye?" Willa looked to him as he now stood at the kitchen entrance. "Cider? Ale?"

"Ale." He lowered to a chair looking on as the kitchen helpers worked. Pots boiled, items were chopped, dough for bread was kneaded. The activity was like a choreographed play, with each person doing their role.

Ella entered and peered down at him. Although young, perhaps a year older than him, she exuded the wisdom of someone much older. Perhaps it was because she'd grown up the only lass in a household of six brothers.

"Something troubles ye," she stated as she lifted a bowl and began stirring. "What is it?"

Padraig lowered his voice. "Will the handfasting be like a marriage?"

"Aye, of course," Ella replied gayly. "Ye will have all the rights that a husband has." She smiled, leaning into his ear, she whispered, "Not to worry, there isn't a bedding ceremony."

He cleared his throat. "What if I do not wish to bed her?"

His sister-in-law frowned. "I am not sure. It may be expected, I suppose. Especially by her father."

Padraig considered that since they would not have to provide proof, they could share a bedchamber without actually becoming intimate.

When Ella poked his shoulder he looked at her.

"Ye are about to do something very foolish."

Why had he done it? Padraig swallowed the last of the ale and stood. "It seems I am." He drank the ale, put the cup down and stood. "I best find a way to distract myself."

FINDING RAURI IN the courtyard, he was glad to have someone to spar with. They practiced until it was almost time for the ceremony. Even then, Rauri had to be the one to remind him to prepare.

"Perhaps ye should wash," his cousin said with a knowing grin. "The pretty lass will not want a man who smells like a swine in her bed otherwise."

Padraig gave him a droll look. "Do ye speak from experience?"

Rauri threw his head back and laughed, making Padraig wish he could be as carefree.

It wasn't that he didn't care for Freya, the problem was that he wasn't sure he would be able to keep from developing more feelings. He did not wish to be tied down yet. There were too many beautiful lasses and the last thing he wanted was to be married to just one.

Something in his chest stirred at thinking that perhaps Freya was the woman for him. Hard as he tried, he could not think of another woman he felt as attracted to.

When he passed the great room, the air was festive. He hurried past before his mother could corral him and make him do something. After a quick swim in the nearby loch, he felt more prepared to face what was ahead. Yet, his stomach tumbled at the thought of what he'd gotten himself into.

He slipped in the front door, hoping to make it past and up the stairs to his bedchamber to relax for a few moments.

"Padraig." Evander's voice stopped him, and he turned to find his brother and Rauri motioning for him to follow them into the study where whiskey was poured, and Evander held his cup up. "That ye find happiness always brother."

Padraig drank down the fiery liquid. "Aye. I thank ye."

"There is still time to change yer mind," Rauri said meeting his gaze. "No shame in making a mistake. Ye could slip out the back and leave."

"He will not," Evander said although he did look toward the door as if considering it. "Padraig will stand by his word."

"Can it not be somewhere besides the chapel?" Padraig asked glancing toward the doorway as well. "This is not to be a true union. I do not wish for it to be done in there."

His brother nodded. "Very well. The ceremony will take place in the great room. Remember brother, a handfasting leaves ye the option of returning the lass before twelve months pass."

THE HANDFASTING WAS done in the great room as he'd requested. Padraig stood before the huge fireplace, moments later Freya walked toward him.

Despite the fact he knew this was being done only as a means to an end, he could not help the tightening in his chest and lump that formed in his throat as she walked toward him. Whoever had styled her hair had done so in a way that flattered her beautiful face.

She wore a dress that he didn't remember but had probably been left by his sister. The gown was a pale green creation that brought out the color of her eyes. Her expression was serene, which he took as a good sign.

His shoulders lowered at noting her hand did not tremble when she placed it next to his on the table that had been set up for the purpose of binding. However, when she looked to him there were so many questions in the green depths, that he had to look away.

"I, Padraig James Macdonald, hereby take ye, Freya Eliza MacLeod," Padraig stated as their wrists were bound by both Lady MacLeod and his mother. "…and thereto plight thee my troth," he finished.

Freya's voice was soft, but strong, as she repeated the vows. It took a moment, but at seeing their hands bound, he realized he'd not placed his over hers. Maneuvering around the binding ribbons, he managed it.

In that moment, when both looked to each other as the clergy said a blessing over them Padraig realized he did indeed wish to remain with her. Freya would not be going back to Harris or to the Scottish shore. But instead she would remain with him forever.

CHAPTER EIGHT

Something Freya had learned in the years of living with her family was that what things looked like on the surface were rarely what was real. She expected that as soon as her relatives left, her life would change dramatically.

It wasn't any outward sign, but there was a strange undertone during the handfasting festivities. Every so often, she noted an exchange of looks between Lady Macdonald and Padraig. At other times, between other members of the Macdonald family. Something was afoot. Perhaps everyone was against the union.

Although it saddened her, Freya was prepared. There in North Uist, she was closer to the Isle of Skye and from there she could easily take a birlinn and reach the western shore of Rona. From there, hopefully she would be able to hire a carriage to get to her aunt's home.

She'd brought all her savings and was more prepared than ever to make her journey.

Throughout the festivities, she could not complain about Padraig's attention. Once again, he turned to her, his face softened by whisky.

"Dance with me."

She'd already explained to him she was not a good dancer, but he'd insisted and in the end showed her some simple steps.

Between his arms, Freya allowed herself to forget everything and pretend that he did indeed care for her, and they'd marry before the year was up. They would live there together, raising a family.

When she stepped on his foot he chuckled, lifted her in his arms, and turned in a circle, to the delight of those in attendance, who clapped and whistled.

"It is time for ye to go to bed." Orla came to her as soon as the song ended. Her sour expression had not changed since earlier when she'd helped her dress. More than once she'd murmured how it should be Iona who was being handfasted.

Freya followed Orla and Ella up the stairs to a different bedchamber than where she'd been staying. In there a beautiful nightdress had been laid on the bed.

"I thought there was not to be a bedding," Freya stated, her heart already hammering.

Ella gave her an apologetic look. "There won't be a bedding ceremony, however, yer father demanded proof of consummation."

"This is a handfasting, not a wedding," Freya replied, her face hot with embarrassment.

Orla gave her a droll look. "Yer father is ensuring Padraig Macdonald is true in his intentions."

With that, the woman walked out.

Ella remained. "Milly will assist ye to get undressed."

As the maid helped Freya out of the gown and brushed her hair out, Ella handed her a small goblet. "Honey mead to settle yer nerves."

"Did ye and yer husband join on yer wedding night?"

Ella smiled. "Aye, and it was wonderful. I am sure ye will

enjoy tonight as well."

Moments later the door closed, and Freya stood in the middle of the room unsure what to do.

It was only moments later that Padraig entered the bedchamber. Dressed in the Macdonald colors of yellow and black, he was stunning. He met her gaze for a long moment and then with purposeful strides crossed the room and took her into his arms.

The kiss was proprietary and immediately Freya was transported into a place of wonderment and passion.

Her nightdress was done away with quickly, his clothing as well. Both naked, he carried her to the bed and placed her upon it. Climbing on the bed, his gaze roamed over her body, but Freya did not feel shy in the least. It was as if this moment was what she'd been waiting for. What her entire existence had been leading to. Being with him.

Of their own volition, her eyes closed when Padraig's hands roamed over her skin, cupping each breast before his lips followed. He sucked at each pert tip sending shivers down to both feet. Freya gasped at the light touches just above the apex of her legs.

The act was so intimate and at the same time not enough. She wanted more, needed something to happen.

Padraig trailed kisses from her breasts down the center of her body, pausing at her stomach to trace circles with his tongue.

Although she wasn't versed in the act of lovemaking, she'd always imagined it would be rough and rudimentary. Nothing of what she currently experienced was at all basic. Instead, it was wonderful.

"Ah!" she gasped when Padraig's mouth moved to her sex, his tongue delving into the most intimate part of her body. With each lick, shudders traveled through her core to the exact spot fire was beginning to consume her.

"Oh, oh, oh," she whispered out the sounds. Unsure what to do with her hands, she gripped the bedding certain she would fly away at any moment as Padraig continued unrelenting at her sex.

One moment she fought against the waves that threatened and the next she was swept away. Everything disappeared, except for bright lights that exploded behind her eyes. Freya grabbed the back of Padraig's head wanting him to not move, but not to continue either. Surely this was what death felt like if it was to paradise that one went.

"Ye are beautiful," Padraig's heated breath blew against her ear. Somehow he'd moved and she'd not noticed. "And ye are mine."

Parting her legs, he settled between them, and prodded once again between them. This time she was powerless to do more than moan as he pushed in slowly. The thickness of his staff was unlike anything she imagined.

He pushed in and before she could get quite used to the feeling he thrust into her.

Freya dug her nails into his shoulders, unsure if it was pain she felt or the surging of another wave of passion. She waited for him to move, her eyes closed.

When he took her mouth, he tasted of her, and Freya was astounded at how erotic it was to know where he'd kissed her.

Padraig began moving, the sensations totally different this time than when his mouth had been there.

"Relax and feel me inside of ye," Padraig instructed.

Freya met his gaze, instantly trusting him. "Aye." She allowed her body to take over. Keeping her eyes open, she felt the wonderful sliding of his member against the walls of her sex, and she watched his every expression as passion began to overtake him. Moment by moment he increased the tempo until their bodies slammed together.

The threat of another wave was intimidating and exciting at the same time. Freya braced for a moment and then let go, allowing it to roll over her as she cried out.

"Oh, Padraig!"

The following afternoon, Freya entered the sitting room to join the Macdonald ladies.

Her family had left that morning. At his departure, her father had hugged her, which was a surprising occurrence. She wasn't sure but could almost swear he looked at her with pride. "Be well daughter. Come visit when ye can."

Orla and Iona had walked past and out the door with barely a word to either her or the Macdonald's. It wasn't surprising.

"How fare ye?" Ella asked with a playful gleam. "I take it ye slept well?"

Freya felt her cheeks warm. "Very well thank ye. Padraig was gone when I woke. I am usually an early riser, so it was surprising."

"This is their hunting day," Lady Macdonald stated with a frown. "One would think he would beg out of it today."

Ella laughed. "He went in hopes of avoiding being ribbed. Little does he know."

D URING THE MIDDAY meal, Padraig, Evander, and Rauri returned.

With a huge bow and quiver on his back, Padraig went directly to her and kissed her brow. "Would ye like to go to the village?"

"Aye, I would," Freya replied with a wide smile. "It would be lovely."

T HE RIDE TO the village was not long. It was a picturesque little town with shops and stalls that they stopped at so that Freya could choose items to purchase. Being she'd not taken much care for her appearance, there were many things she needed.

When at a stall that sold hair combs and ribbons, she painstakingly picked out three. "These are beautiful," she told the smiling woman who held out a comb that matched her selections.

Freya looked to Padraig. "I do not wish to spend too much."

He took the comb from the woman and placed it next to the ribbons she'd selected. Then he took one of each ribbon the woman had, several combs, a handheld mirror, and several hairpins and added them to the pile. "Anything else ye suggest?" he asked the woman who was now beaming.

In the end, the carriage was overloaded with their purchases. Bags, slippers, sandals, and boots were among what Padraig had her choose. As well as two shawls, some perfumed oils and a pair of bracelets.

Freya was overwhelmed. She'd never been made to feel so special.

"How about we stop at the tavern for meat pies? The owner's wife makes the best."

"I doubt anyone could cook better than Willa," Freya said.

"True," Padraig replied. "However, these meat pies will make ye wonder."

They sat in the tavern and ate while he told her how he and Evander had downed a buck that morning.

"My sisters hated that we went hunting all the time, as they wished to be escorted here or to a festival." He shook his head. "Sometimes at overhearing their plans, we purposely went out."

Freya sighed. "I hope to meet them." She left the words *before I leave* unsaid. Freya was sure she'd not been wrong about the fact something was afoot. She would let a day or two pass and then ask Padraig. First, she would enjoy these days and pretend all was well.

"Aye, they visit often. Isobel is married to the Ross and Beatrice to his brother, Duncan. Ye remind me more of Isobel, who is intelligent and quiet. Beatrice is a whirlwind."

Already she wanted to meet them. "I hope they like me."

"Judging by how much Ella and my mother already do, have no doubts."

As they headed home, in the distance birlinns bobbed on the shoreline looking like fish out of water.

"Do they all belong to Clan Macdonald?" Freya asked watching men guide the vessels away and toward the docks.

"Nay. Some are manned by men who take passengers to Skye and beyond. Most are returning now as they leave at first daylight."

The ride back seemed to take forever since Padraig kissed her breathless every few minutes making her anxious to be alone with him.

"How much longer to the keep?" Freya asked breathlessly.

By the playful look in his eyes and deep chuckle, he knew exactly why she asked. "Not soon enough."

IT WAS LATE one day a fortnight later that Freya entered the kitchen to find Willa sitting at the table with a cup of warm cider. The woman looked up from her cup and smiled. "Can I get ye something?"

"No. I came to see if I could help with what is planned for last meal and to talk to ye about something." Freya sat and looked at the woman who shrugged.

"All has been prepared for last meal. Stew is boiling, the flatbread will be prepared just before."

As the days passed, Freya had forgotten about the strange sensation at the handfasting. Everyone was lovely to her, seeming to accept her as part of the family. She'd never been happier.

Freya went to the window. "I would like to plant herbs in a portion of the garden. Is there space for it?"

They discussed the pros and cons of each side of the large garden plot finally coming to a decision that Freya could use a side that received shaded sunlight most of the day, which most of her herbs required. Delighted, she went outside to find a spot and plan for her plantings.

The wind was becoming brisk, noting that soon fall would arrive and bring with it cooler air. If she were to plant herbs, it was best to do so soon so that she would have time to grow and harvest before the weather became too cold.

Picking up a stick, she began drawing in the dirt, first outlining the length and width and then straight lines to where she'd plant different herbs.

Male voices caught her attention. One sounded like Padraig. Not wishing to eavesdrop, bending back over, she continued on with her task.

"It seems yer handfasting is going well," a male, who she recognized as Rauri stated.

Padraig did not reply. At this point, Freya lowered to the ground and paid closer attention.

"Has yer plan changed then?" Rauri asked.

"I am not sure as yet," Padraig finally replied. "I must think on it."

Rauri grunted. "Ye cannot continue to bed the lass if ye plan to send her off to find her family. What if she becomes with child?"

Again Padraig was silent.

Breath caught in her chest as she waited for his response. Waited for him to tell Rauri he did not plan to send her away, but to marry her at the end of the handfasting period. Without prodding, tears trailed down her cheeks.

Padraig's reply was said in a strange tone. As if he fought for what to say. "She does not deserve to be mistreated by me after all she's gone through."

What did that mean? Why had he not declared his intentions to marry her? Freya almost jumped up to demand an answer, but her body folded into itself. Pain like nothing she'd ever felt slicing through her entire body.

She lay in the dirt, not caring that she wore a beautiful dress. One that she'd worn in hopes of being pleasing to him.

What a fool she was.

CHAPTER NINE

THE SUN BARELY peeked from the horizon when Freya arrived at the shore. Wearing one of her older dresses, and not bothering to comb her hair, hopefully no one would recognize her. She pulled the hood down low over her face as she paid the price asked.

With the bundle that she'd packed before leaving Harris between her feet, Freya kept an anxious eye toward the keep on the hill hoping her absence was not noted until well after she reached Rona, a small isle just past Skye.

She'd never told anyone exactly where her mother's sister lived. Her father had told her he thought it to be on Scotland's coast or on Skye. She'd read letters and knew they resided on the tiny isle that no one paid much notice to.

If not for the horrible tightness in her chest, Freya would smile at her ingenuity. No one would think to look for her on Rona, especially not Padraig. Not that she expected that he'd ever come after her. After all, his plan was to send her away.

In the days that followed her overhearing the conversation, she'd tried to figure out why he'd asked for her to remain. In his own way, he'd wished to rescue her from mistreatment.

If only he'd told her the truth from the beginning. That he wanted to help her get away and be with her family.

Milly, the maid, had finally told her that she'd overheard

Padraig's plan to help her. The maid spoke thinking Freya would be pleased, as she wasn't aware of the second part of the plan. Padraig planned to help her find her family before the handfasting time was over.

As the bìrlinn left the docking, the slender vessel cut through the sea easily. Thanks to coins she'd gotten from Padraig as spending money, she was able to purchase passage and still have plenty left. She'd easily be able to get to Rona and find her family, without touching her own savings.

Hours passed until finally the man announced they'd reached the small isle. Along with a young man—who'd left North Uist to return home—she climbed out of the bìrlinn.

Freya stood by as the two men unloaded everything the young man had purchased. Obviously, he'd been on a trip to procure necessities for his family. Finally, they said their farewells to the man, who waved them away.

"Where are ye headed miss?" the young man asked. On the way there, he'd told her he had a cart and horse and offered to take her where she was going.

"My aunt, Mairead Anderson, do ye know her?" It was a silly question as there were only two families who lived on the tiny isle. The Andersons and the Browns.

"Aye. I can take ye there. Her youngest daughter is married to my brother, Nathan." The young man bobbed his head enthusiastically.

Moments later, they rode along a narrow road that led to a village of about five cottages. The young man slowed and pointed to a sole cottage up a hill. "That is yer aunt's home."

"I can walk from here," Freya told him. He helped her down from the wagon and she grabbed the two bundles she'd packed.

Meeting his gaze, she handed him a coin. "Thank ye."

As Freya walked past two cottages, people watched her with curiosity, but no one asked her anything. Such were the people of the remote isles. She remembered her mother telling her how they kept to themselves and were very wary of newcomers.

The woman who opened the cottage door was too young to be her aunt, but by the similar looks, Freya thought her to be one of the daughters.

"I am Freya, my mother was called Rowena Anderson. I am looking for Mairead Anderson." Freya's voice shook as the woman looked her over. Then her face broke into a smile. "I am yer cousin, Rowena, named after yer mother."

"Rowena?" Freya's voice hitched at remembering her cousin who'd come to visit several times before her mother died. Rowena hugged her tightly. "Aye 'tis me. Come in and tell me what has happened."

Upon entering her aunt came out from a room and studied her for only a moment before she began crying. "Ye look so much like yer mother."

Before long she was treated to a meal, wrapped in a blanket since the small cottage was quite drafty, and was surrounded by her other cousins who'd been called over.

Slowly, she told them about her life in Harris. About the mistreatment and finally about the handfasting.

"He planned to send ye away?" her aunt stated with a frown. "Men are without care. What if ye came to be with child? What then? Raise the bairn on yer own?" Her aunt stood and stomped to the door as if Padraig was to appear any moment and peered out.

Rowena glared past the doorway. "I am glad ye left. He does not deserve ye."

Freya smiled at her cousin. "Can I stay here for now? Until I find a place."

"Ye will stay here as long as ye wish. 'Tis only me living here now, my husband, yer uncle Harold, is gone. Two years past. God bless him." Her aunt gave her a knowing look. "Once ye get past yer broken heart, ye will find joy in the simple life here. And no one will mistreat ye here lass."

It was a long time before everyone began trickling out. Young ones lingered running and playing outside the doorway.

"Come, Freya." Her aunt called her to the small kitchen. "The bairns will not leave until I make them sweet tarts."

Side by side, they cooked while her aunt told her of life there on Rona. There were only about a hundred people who braved life on the small isle. They had to travel to Skye and Uist for most supplies. Therefore the people were quite handy and able to make most things for themselves.

Small gardens dotted the landscape as they grew what they could before the weather became too cold. Once winter set in, times became lean. However, according to her aunt, they came together as a community to purchase goats and pigs, so that they would have meat and milk.

"I wish I could have come sooner," Freya said as they cleaned up. "This is where I belong."

For a long moment her aunt studied her. "Whatever comes lass. We are yer family and will be here for ye."

Her eyes burned with unshed tears at the words. Freya

prayed not to be with child. If she was, she would accept and love it, of course. However, she preferred not to have a permanent reminder of Padraig.

When the first week passed, then the second, Freya stopped looking to the shore whenever a birlinn came into view. Padraig would not come for her. In a way she was glad because it would sadden her to decide between the family that accepted her without question and the man she loved.

By the end of the third week, Freya panicked. Her courses had yet to come, and she was sure it had to be time. At night she prayed for them to come, hoping not to have to give birth to a child who would grow up without a father.

By the fourth week, her prayers changed. She asked God for a healthy child who would grow up loved and cherished.

CHAPTER TEN

"Ye plan to leave again?" Evander asked at seeing Padraig appear wearing a thick cloak, fur boots, and with his sword across his back. "Where to now?"

"Skye again and then perhaps another of the surrounding isles. The bìrlinn owners have said not to have taken a woman alone to mainland Scotland, nor to Skye, but where else could she be?"

After waiting two weeks, he'd finally sent a spy to Harris. They'd found out Freya was not there.

"It could be she is still here in North Uist," his mother said. "Perhaps hiding in a village."

"We would have found her by now," Padraig stated. "We keep going in circles. I do not understand how she got away without being stopped and how no one seems to have seen her anywhere."

His brother shook her head. "It could be someone took her. The MacLeods of the north may have found out about her being here. They hate the man, so it would be a way to get back at him."

"I have considered it," Padraig said. "If they did, no one saw them. I do not see how they could have done it."

Ella entered the room. "If it were me and I overheard yer plan to do away with me, I would have left as well." She gave

Padraig a pointed look. "I would hide if I saw ye or any Macdonald coming."

Despite the tang of anger at himself, Padraig managed to keep from storming out of the room. He let out a calming breath. "Where would ye go if ye were in her place?"

"I would disguise myself as a peasant, hire a birlinn, and go to family. I would hope that once they found out what I have been through they would not allow anyone near me."

Evander stared at his wife. "She could have spoken to Padraig and cleared matters before leaving. If that is what she did."

Ella gave her husband a sharp look. "No. It was Padraig who should have spoken to her." She whirled toward him. "Ye should have explained what ye planned from the beginning and given her the choice of whether or not to lay with ye. What if she is with child?"

His temper flared. "That is why I am looking for her. Because I wish to beg her to forgive me. Whether or not she is with child, I want her back. I wish to marry her."

The silence that followed was broken by a clearing of a throat.

After being gone for several days to search for Freya, his cousin Rauri walked in. "I found her."

At the three words, a weight was lifted from Padraig's shoulders. He let out a long breath. "Wh-where is she?"

"With her family, the Andersons of Rona. She is living with her aunt. From what I hear, she is well and seems happy. Are ye sure to want to take her from there?"

He was already headed to the door, but the question stopped him. He turned. "Why would I not?"

"Ye and she are not married. Yer plan all along was to send her to her family. She went herself and now seems quite content. She lives with her aunt and is surrounded by family. According to the lass I spoke to, Freya shares a well sized cottage and has taken up teaching the family bairns to plant herb gardens."

"I would ask how ye found out so much, but I would probably rather not know." His mother gave her nephew a knowing look.

"Met a bonnie lass at a tavern…" Rauri started, stopped, and chuckled at the look his aunt gave him. "Aye, it is best I do not say."

THE COLD WIND blew across the birlinn making Padraig pull his cloak tighter. The weather had changed recently from a comfortable warmth to quite cold. As the vessel cut through the choppy gray water, he kept his gaze forward wishing to spot the small isle first.

Since leaving to come, he'd wrestled with what to say that would convince Freya to return to him. He would tell her the truth. His misguided way of wanting to help her and then how he'd fallen in love and planned to marry her. He would apologize profusely for not stating that to Rauri when she'd overheard them talking. If only he'd known she was there.

It had been almost two months since she'd left, and he'd missed her every single day. Their bed felt empty and cold without her small form next to him.

"It is there," Rauri called out pointing to the shore that came into view. "We have arrived."

He and his cousin helped the two men who'd sailed the

vessel to pull it up to the shore. Everyone would remain with the birlinn while he went to search out Freya. Although his cousin offered to come along, Padraig did not want to have a witness if she turned him away.

As he walked down the main street, several villagers watched him with ill-concealed animosity. He wondered if they'd already figured who he was.

At seeing an older man guiding a small flock of sheep down from a hill, he hurried to the man. "Can ye tell me where Mairead Anderson lives?"

The old man's eyes narrowed. "Ye should go back the way ye came." Then he spit at the ground and walked off shooing the animals to go faster.

Obviously, no one would help him. Padraig continued forward, following the unclear directions the lass at the tavern had given Rauri. Moments later, he caught sight of a young lad racing up a hill. The boy looked over his shoulder at him and ran faster.

Someone had sent the boy to alert Freya.

The race was on. Padraig dropped his heavy cloak and ran to catch up with the boy. Despite the lad's swiftness, Padraig quickly caught up with him and grabbed him by the tunic.

He gave the boy two coins and pushed him back toward the village. "Go away."

Seeming torn, the lad finally decided the coins were worth whatever scolding he'd receive at not relaying the message. He scampered off after pointing out the cottage where Freya lived.

Upon arriving, Padraig slowed and studied the structure. It was as described. The cottage was large, and the thatched roof recently redone. The walls were thick and there was a large garden on one side and a pen with livestock on the other.

Chickens scurried away when he approached the front door, their loud clucking alerting those inside of his presence.

The door opened and a woman who resembled Freya stood in the opening. Her hands went to her hips and her eyes narrowed.

"Ye must be Padraig Ross. The man who broke my niece's heart. Away with ye." She made a shooing motion as if he were a pesky fly. "Go on. She has no need of ye."

"I have a need of her," Padraig replied. "I have good intentions. I did not plan to send her away. She misunderstood…" He spoke loudly hoping Freya was inside and could hear him.

"I do not think she misunderstood. What I think is that ye feel guilty for what ye did," the woman said and then seemed to soften. "I do not think ye are a bad man, Padraig Ross. But I do know that if ye truly cared for her, ye would not have let her go."

"Ye are right," Padraig stated. "I do feel badly. Especially as I was not sure of my feelings for her at the time. I have never been in love before ye see. It was confusing and I acted without thought. Allow me to speak to her. I want her to come home with me."

"That place was never my home." Freya appeared behind her aunt. If possible, she looked more beautiful than he remembered. Her face was soft, as if she'd come into her own. Freya's loose hair fell in waves around her shoulders. When her gaze met his, there was a sort of peace about them. As if she held no anger, but no there was no affection either.

"I forgive ye Padraig. Ye do not have to feel badly about me. I am well."

"Can I speak to ye for a moment?"

At Freya's nod, the woman motioned for him to enter,

then went out of the room.

"I wish to marry ye Freya," Padraig said reaching to touch her, but lowering his arm when she leaned away. "I am in love with ye. I wish I could change the way things happened."

She moved closer and peered up at him, searching his face as if to see if he spoke the truth. "I cannot return with ye. I do not feel as if it is where I should be at this moment."

"Freya, please."

"Go Padraig. When the time is right, if I feel that I should be with ye, then I will come to ye. Do not seek me out again. Please go."

When he leaned forward and pressed his lips to hers, she allowed it, her eyelids falling closed.

"Please go," she whispered.

Never in his life had Padraig felt so low as when he trudged back down the hill to where his cloak lay on the ground. His chest was tight making breathing hard. The cold wind made the trail of tears on his face feel like ice. And yet he could not stop them from falling.

Love was so many things, his mother had once told him. It was holding on to people tightly and at the same time knowing when to let them go. For him, it was the latter. He loved Freya enough to let her go.

When another month passed, Padraig lost hope of Freya returning.

One afternoon, he and Evander trudged through the forest in the falling rain hunting in silence. They'd not shot any game that day. It could be that neither of them had even tried.

At the sight of a deer, Padraig lifted his bow, set the arrow, and pulled back. The deer turned, its eyes meeting his for just a blink, then it scampered into the woods. He lowered the bow.

"Ye missed," Evander said dryly.

"Why are we out here freezing our bullocks off?" Padraig finally asked. "We should head back."

Evander grinned. "Because ye needed to get outside and work things out. Yer heart is broken, but perhaps it is time for ye to move forward. Mother has asked that we arrange a bride for ye."

"Why do mothers think marriage is a solution to every man's problem?" Padraig stepped on a branch, the sound of it breaking loud in the quiet forest.

"Sometimes it is the solution. In this case, I may have to agree. Ye cannot continue walking about the keep and staring out the window looking forlorn."

Padraig gave his brother a droll look. "I go on daily patrols, I train with the guards, and have gone to the tavern. In other words, I do what I've always done."

"Ye have gone to the tavern once and that was only because Rauri wanted ye to meet his lass. The other things, aye ye have done this or that, but ye must admit to not being the same."

Running his hand down his now long beard, Padraig shrugged. "I am not getting married. Ye and mother may as well accept it."

They continued in silence, turning back to the keep empty-handed. There wasn't a reason really to kill any game as there was plenty of meat at the keep. Someone had killed a wild hog earlier that week and it had been butchered; the meat taken to several poor families in the village.

Their mother waved to them as they returned. She stood at the main house's entry with an expectant look. "Hurry Padraig. Someone is here to see ye."

He looked around the courtyard for a carriage. If his mother had brought someone for him to court, Padraig wasn't sure to be able to keep his temper in check.

"Who is it Mother? I do not wish to be matched up for marriage."

"Ye may change yer mind," his mother said with a sly grin. She then put both hands on his chest and stopped him. "Wash yer face and rinse that horrible beard before coming inside." She motioned toward the stables, where a barrel of fresh rainwater promised a cold experience for his already chilled bones.

"Fine."

His boots were leaden as he made his way into the great room. He hesitated at the entry for a moment to ensure a warm expression. After all, whoever awaited him wasn't to blame that his mother wanted to play matchmaker.

Upon entering, the room was empty except for a woman who warmed her hands at the fireplace.

He considered for a second that she stood at the exact spot where he and Freya had been handfasted.

"Why are ye alone?" he asked keeping his gaze on her hands and not looking at her face. Padraig walked closer at noting that she seemed familiar to him. However, her hair hung down blocking his view of her face.

Unlike Freya, this woman was a bit curvier, her midsection fuller. But she was the same height and her hair the same color. His mother should not have considered someone who would remind him of her.

"I came alone because I was convinced by my aunt that our child had a right to be raised with his father."

Freya turned to meet his gaze, her expression unreadable. "I must agree."

His body refused to listen to his orders to move and he remained planted to the spot where he'd stopped. Neither his legs nor feet responded when he tried to move closer. It seemed the ability to speak was also gone because he opened his mouth and closed it, nary a sound emanating.

His woman straightened and clasped her hands in front of her chest. "That is if ye will have me. If ye truly do care for me."

Finally he was able to move. Although he feared that his heart would burst from his chest. "Freya…" He rushed forward, wrapped his arms around her, and brought her against his chest. "Freya."

Despite himself, he could not keep the tears of happiness at bay. "Ye have returned to me," he whispered holding her tightly.

"Ye are smothering me," Freya said pushing back and he loosened his hold but did not fully release her. "Aye, I have returned."

Obviously his family stood within earshot because moments later, his mother, Ella, Evander, and even Rauri entered. Everyone was smiling broadly.

His heart could barely stand it. The fact that not only the love of his life had returned to him, but also that his family was happy for him.

"If Da were here, he would be very glad for ye right now," Evander said. "I am very glad not to have my brother moping about any longer," he continued looking to Freya.

Freya looked to him. "I was sad as well. Could not stop thinking about ye."

"We must celebrate." His mother wiped an errant tear. "Bring honeyed mead," she said to a pair of maids who looked on with wide smiles. "And tonight we will feast."

THAT NIGHT, THEY lay next to each other, it was hard for Padraig to believe Freya was there with him. He ran his hand over the small swell of her stomach marveling at the thought that soon he would have a son.

"We must marry immediately," Padraig said. "My son will not be born a bastard."

"We are handfasted and therefore he will not be considered such," Freya said pressing a kiss to his cheek. "And ye know it could be a daughter."

Padraig kissed the place where his hand had been. "Ye are a lad are ye not?" he whispered against her belly.

Lifting to look at Freya, he met her gaze. "I hope one day ye will love me as much as I love ye."

She nodded, her eyes misting.

When he took her mouth with his, Padraig fought not to be overly passionate. It was to be their first time since she'd gone, and he wished to convey how much he cared for her.

The skin under his palms was soft as silk as he slid her nightdress off. Freya assisted by lifting her hips and then her arms so that he could easily undress her.

The kiss deepened and he brought her against his already bare body. When she wrapped her arms around him, joy filled his heart.

"Take me Padraig," she murmured against his mouth. "I need ye."

Positioning himself at her entrance, Padraig guided his hardness and slid into her warm wet sex. She was tight around him making it difficult to keep from losing control and coming too soon.

Padraig pulled out and then drove back in, his body taking over. Over and over, he thrust into her, both of them lost in the moment. Freya's nails dug into his bottom as she prodded him to move faster and take her higher.

It was only with her that he'd ever felt intoxicated with passion to the point where the noises that erupted from his throat—a mixture of a moan and a growl—sounded strange to his ears.

When she began to shake, she threw her head back and a loud cry erupted. Only then did Padraig allow himself to let go. And it was wonderful, heat that had collected between his legs surged up his back and down both legs.

He managed two more thrusts before release came so hard, he was lost.

"I love ye Padraig." The words were like a soft balm to his overwrought senses and Padraig collapsed, pushing his face into the bedding beside her so she would not see his tears.

EPILOGUE

Caden Padraig MacDonald was born on a sunny May afternoon. Padraig strutted around the keep, his feet barely touching the ground at becoming the father of a healthy son.

A month later, the MacLeod came to visit.

"Yer grandson," Freya said handing the bundled bairn to her father.

He looked at her for a long moment before peering at the child in his arms. "He resembles both ye and Padraig", he finally said.

Freya nodded. "Aye, I believe so as well."

In almost a year since she'd left Harris, it was the first time her father had come to see her. Her father placed the bairn into a blanket that had been set in a crib near the fireplace. They were in the sitting room upstairs, just the three of them.

"I wished to see ye," her father said, his word stilted. "To tell ye that I was wrong to allow Orla and Iona to mistreat ye all those years. I should have put a stop to it, not allow it to go on for so long."

The statement made Freya suspicious. It wasn't like her father to ever care about her, or anyone other than himself for that matter. "Why do ye say it now? It is all in the past now. I do my best not to think about it."

His face fell. "I have done so many things I am repentant for. I have sent men to seek yer brother. They have not found him as yet. I need to make amends to both of ye. It has become apparent to me how much ye did to keep our home well run. Without ye the house is not the same."

Freya didn't understand what had occurred to bring her father to seek her out. A part of her felt that he needed her to tell him she was happy and treated well.

"I am happy, Father. Padraig is a good husband, and the family has accepted me fully. The bairn and I have everything we need and more. I am sure my brother will return when he is ready. I pray for Connor every day. In the end, all will be well. For me, things turned out nicely."

"I am glad." Her father looked down at the sleeping bairn. "I hear there is to be a wedding today."

"Aye, I am glad ye are here to celebrate with us."

His father stood. "I must meet with Evander. I have decided to allow the people in the northern region their freedom. I heard he has already set a treaty in motion. Yer brother-in-law is a good laird."

THE GREAT ROOM was alight with lanterns hanging on every wall and candelabras on the tables. The bride and groom, Rauri and Giarda, the tavern owner's daughter, were married that day. Music played and food was plentiful.

Freya met Padraig's gaze and smiled as both recalled that just a few months earlier, their wedding had been celebrated there.

Just like this day, the clan celebrated the beginning of married life for a new couple.

When Rauri led his new wife to dance, others immediately joined in. Padraig's mother danced while rocking the cooing Caden, who seemed to take delight in the music.

"Dance with me," Padraig whispered in her ear. "Then perhaps we can steal away while Mother is preoccupied with the bairn."

Freya laughed as her husband led her to dance, twirling in his arms, happiness overtaking her.

From his seat at the front table her father looked on, his lips curving at seeing that Freya finally did get the happy ending she very much deserved.

He looked to the ceiling thinking that perhaps her mother looked down upon their daughter feeling the same happiness he did.

Get to know the Ross Clan by reading The Heartless Laird. It's a fun, action filled story that will keep you engrossed. Happy Reading Friend!

A Note to Readers

Let's get to know one another,

Sign up for my newsletter and get a free Clan Ross story!

Newsletter Link: https://bit.ly/3vSEbYY.

I sent out my newsletter monthly which includes book news, giveaways and sneak peeks!

About the Author

Enticing. Engaging. Romance.

USA Today Bestselling Author Hildie McQueen writes strong brooding alphas who meet their match in feisty brave heroines. If you like stories with a mixture of passion, drama, and humor, you will love Hildie's storytelling where love wins every single time!

A fan of all things pink, Paris, and four-legged creatures, Hildie resides in eastern Georgia, USA, with her super-hero husband Kurt and three little yappy dogs.

Visit her website at www.hildiemcqueen.com.

Printed in Great Britain
by Amazon